SHORT CUTS

INTRODUCTIONS TO FILM STUDIES

WAR CINEMA

HOLLYWOOD ON THE FRONT LINE

GUY WESTWELL

WALLFLOWER

LONDON and NEW YORK

A Wallflower Paperback

First published in Great Britain in 2006 by
Wallflower Press
6a Middleton Place, Langham Street, London W1W 7TE
www.wallflowerpress.co.uk

A catalogue record for this book is available from the British Library

ISBN 1 904764 54 1

Book design by Rob Bowden Design

Printed in Great Britain by Antony Rowe Ltd, Chippenham, Wiltshire

CONTENTS

ACKNOWLEDGEMENTS

The writing of this book was made possible through a Research Leave Award granted by the Arts and Humanities Research Council. I am particular grateful to Jesse Edwards, Ian Craven and Robert Rosenstone for their help with the funding application. Thank you to Yoram Allon, and all the team at Wallflower Press, for their invaluable editorial work and general support. I am indebted to Mark Bedford, John Gillot, Debora Marletta and Suzi Westwell for finding time in their busy lives for intelligent and helpful engagement with the manuscript. Thanks also to Isil Mete, who is the kind of dedicated and generous student that makes teaching Film Studies at London Metropolitan University such a rewarding experience. Much gratitude and love must go to Richard Crownshaw and Deborah Slaughter, two close friends whose inspired decision to relocate to Sydney, Australia for six months, and allow me to join them, made this book possible. Surf's up, dudes! Last, but certainly not least, much love to Debora for all her love, laughter and support.

INTRODUCTION

The war movie is as old as the cinema itself, and from early experiments through to today's high-concept blockbusters, war has been a staple Hollywood product. War movies lend shape and structure to war, identifying enemies, establishing objectives and allowing audiences to vicariously experience the danger and excitement of the front line. For America, the war movie was central to the global propaganda campaigns waged during World War I and World War II, it provided therapeutic aid in the aftermath of the divisive and traumatising experience of losing the war in Vietnam, and, more recently, a significant cycle of big-budget productions (of which *Saving Private Ryan* (1999) is probably the best known) has made an Americanised version of World War II a key touchstone for American national identity.

The centrality of the war movie to the cultural imagination of war can be seen clearly in contemporary war cinema. For example, in the immediate aftermath of the 11 September 2001 terrorist attacks, Karl Rove, senior advisor to President George Bush Jr, met with several top Hollywood executives to discuss how the film industry might contribute to the 'war on terror'. As a result of this meeting *Black Hawk Down* (2001) and *We Were Soldiers* (2002), films with clear patriotic and pro-military tendencies, had their release dates brought forward in order to cash in on, and help to consolidate, post-11 September bellicosity. At the same time, the release date of *Buffalo Soldiers* (2003), a story of heroin dealing on a US military base in West Germany in 1989, and *The Quiet American* (2002), which tells of America's clandestine support of terrorist networks in Vietnam in the 1950s, had their release dates delayed because they were deemed too

critical of the US military. As these examples indicate, the Bush administration considered Hollywood a way of gaining important leverage in the
construction of a way of thinking about war that would support and sustain
a more aggressive foreign policy stance. Further, Hollywood executives saw
a favourable business opportunity exploitable via the fine-tuning of their
release schedules in order to tap into the belligerent public mood. These
two attuned actions reinforced one another and reconciled the short-term
political interests of the state with the connected cycles of capitalist production and consumption that define the film industry. The result: a cycle
of Hollywood movies (all released in close proximity to the start of the war
in Afghanistan) with, as this book will demonstrate, significant pro-war
tendencies. In fact, it is common for a tacit agreement to be made not to
criticise the state during times of significant foreign policy commitment (a
process referred to as 'rallying around the flag') and studies have shown
that in every war since World War II (including the conflict in Vietnam) the
media, including the film industry, has provided both implicit and explicit
support for war (see Hallin 1986 and Knightley 1989).

The thoroughly entangled relationship between war, movies about war
and the cultural imagination of war is even more pronounced if we look
back further to the propagandist role played by the cinema during World
War II. Working under the aegis of a government agency, the Office of War
Information (OWI), key film industry personnel including well-known film
directors such as John Ford, Frank Capra and William Wyler joined the
armed forces and contributed their skills to the propaganda campaign.
The films they produced – *December 7th* (1943), the *Why We Fight* series
(1943–45) and *Memphis Belle* (1944) to name but a few – were all carefully
designed to help America wage war more effectively by manufacturing
consent for the stated policy goals of the nation. These films demonstrate
how, in a democracy, the manufacture of popular support for war is a
logistical necessity without which the nation's war-making capacity is
severely hampered. Most critics agree that the war movie genre was given
its distinct and lasting shape during this period of national emergency and
insomuch as the genre still conforms to this generic template it necessarily
– almost by default – will tend to corroborate any general or specific rallying cry to war.

War movies also imbricate with the military-industrial complex on a
number of further levels. The majority of the war movies I shall consider

in this book were made with the explicit support of the American military in a partnership referred to by Hollywood studio executives as 'mutual exploitation'. The mutuality in this arrangement stems from the Pentagon's willingness to provide military hardware and personnel (thereby slashing production budgets) in exchange for favourable representation. As a result, when we watch a war movie we should always try to remember that, even within the demarcated realm of fantasy and escape that is the cinema, what we are seeing on screen is the actual apparatus of war: real airplanes, real warships, real uniforms, even real soldiers who frequently act as extras and advisers. This arrangement is long-lived and was worked out as early as 1918, when D. W. Griffith's World War I propaganda film *Hearts of the World* was given financial backing by the British high command.

Therefore, the armed forces have considerable power in shaping scripts and will often withdraw support if a film is perceived to be unflattering. Lawrence Suid's description of the complex negotiations that shaped the pre-production of *From Here to Eternity* (1953) show how James Jones' controversial novel, an insider account of the US military on the eve of World War II, was given a makeover to reduce its critical bite and placate the Pentagon (1978: 117–29). In courting the favour of the military, an institution with a significant vested interest in war, Hollywood tends to produce movies that are, to put it crudely, pro-war. That is, for all their protestations to the contrary, Hollywood movies tend to show war as necessary, if not essential, and present the armed forces as efficient, egalitarian and heroic institutions. Shaped ideologically, through the legacy of the propagandist role of the war movie, and industrially, through the synergy between the military and the film industry, war is almost always shown in a positive light.

The symbiotic relationship between the military and the movies goes even further. The release of a successful Hollywood war movie will often boost recruitment to the US armed forces, with the film functioning as a kind of trailer to encourage civilians into war (*Top Gun* (1986) famously eased a recruitment crisis in the US Navy in the mid-1980s). Furthermore, the American military consider the movies to be essential to the maintenance of good morale within the armed forces, with cinema spaces quickly set up in war zones. In fact, one of the markers of a successfully controlled area is that the area is safe enough to sustain a cinema and a regular programme of screenings (Doherty 1993: 75–6).

In this respect the war cinema is as essential to the waging of war as an M-16 automatic rifle, an aircraft carrier, or a helicopter gunship. Or, as Paul Virilio puts it, 'images have turned into ammunition' (quoted in Armitage 2000: 45). As such, going to the cinema to watch the latest big-budget war movie is an activity at some level implicated in the violence of past and present wars. It is for this reason that I ask the reader at the outset to leave aside their understanding of the war movie as simply entertainment, or even as a form of realist representation holding a mirror to war, and instead to think about the war movie as offering a set of indices to war proper. It is only through this *indexical* relationship between the war movie and war proper, a relationship that is complex, indirect and contradictory, and yet also constitutive, that we can glimpse and begin to articulate the interconnectedness of war, movies about war, and the cultural imagination of war more generally.

The cultural imagination of war

Initial hopes that the end of the Cold War would herald an era of peace have dissolved in the face of vicious conflicts in the former Soviet Union, in south-eastern Europe, and in central and eastern Africa. As I write, the US occupation of Iraq remains bloody and intractable and the 'war on terror' – in pursuit of the dispersed, ill-defined forces of al-Qaeda – pervades further and further into the fabric of things. As well as present-day conflict, the recent past is shaped by the experience of the Cold War, a deadly stand-off between two competing ideological systems predicated on mutually assured destruction and nuclear holocaust. The Cold War's battlefronts were scattered and its military engagements cloaked. Yet the legacies of wars in Korea, Cuba and Vietnam and the after-effects of bitter revolution and counter-revolution in Latin America, Africa and the Middle East, still actively shape the present.

Many people suffer the direct effects of these wars and their legacies but in America and the West more generally, for all but a tiny minority of soldiers, aid workers and military contractors, war remains safely beyond the horizon, something that happens to others. It is true that the terrorist attacks on New York and Washington on 11 September 2001 brought the violence of war closer to the American homeland. However, these terrorist acts – vicious and unconscionable – are ultimately different in nature to the

The cinema as a technology of war: the Twentieth Century Fox logo

effects of war proper, in which catastrophic violence leads to the ruination of economies, the breakdown of law and order, the loss of land and property, and the dislocation of family and community. This experience of war, something all too familiar to people living in Afghanistan or Iraq, is, in the West, only imagined from afar.

In trying to apprehend wars that are far away, often in parts of the world that are remote and alien, Americans are reliant on what might be called the cultural imagination of war. This is shaped by myriad representations of war appearing in numerous contexts, ranging from television news broadcasts, newspaper articles, photojournalism and magazine features to film and television documentaries, comic books, novels, web pages, art exhibitions and war memorials. These representations provide the common ground upon which a collective, shared sense of war is worked out, articulated and sometimes contested. With time, this collected sense of war becomes a pattern of thought, a hard-wired set of expectations and desires that constrain the very ways we think about war.

The cultural imagination of war is complex, the sum of an array of characters, scenarios, vignettes, points of view and narrative structures, gathered together from the various representations listed above. In this book I will be focusing on just one of these representations, the Hollywood war movie. I am interested primarily in those movies where Hollywood puts itself on the front line. It is in these movies – trying to show a known event, often helped directly by the US military – that the cultural imagination of war can be most clearly seen. Each chapter consists of readings of individual Hollywood films, with each individual film chosen as representative of a distinct cycle of films. I wish to argue that these films are reifications of the ideological structures that arbitrate our experience and understanding of war and are hard evidence with which to build a profile of the cultural imagination of war.

This way of thinking about war and representation relies on a particular conceptualisation of ideology. Ideology is a word that has attracted many different definitions and uses but throughout this book I take it to mean the inherited and shared sense of the world held by a people (what Benedict Anderson (1983) terms an 'imagined community') within a particular time and place, and as evidenced by their attitudes, habits, feelings and assumptions. Terry Eagleton – in a useful digest of the complex critical literature on the subject – notes how 'this politically innocuous meaning of ideology comes close to the notion of "world view", in the sense of a relatively well-systematised set of categories which provide a "frame" for the belief, perception and conduct of a body of individuals' (1991: 43). Conceptualised in this way the *framework* offered by the war movie provides the viewer with a particular way of thinking and feeling about war and this constitutes a key element in the over-arching ideology of any imagined community.

In Marxist critical discourse ideology is often perceived to be providing cover for some deeper-seated reality only barely visible beneath ideology's cloak (see Eagleton 1991: 10–26). For example, the explicit propagandist designs that governed the cultural imagination of war during World War I insisted that war be understood in relation to a chivalric code of honour, a Christian rhetoric of sacrifice and a powerful discourse of nationalism. These tropes (so central to the war cinema of the 1910s and 1920s) were used to disguise the imperialist design of a war waged between competing colonial powers. According to this way of thinking the ideological function of the cultural imagination of war is to make war *feel* right. That is, ideology, through the deployment of a specific way of imagining war, encourages us to think of war as a productive mechanism of progressive political change tied, in this instance, to codes of honour, self-sacrifice and national esteem. In doing so we are discouraged from questioning why and how so much life was wasted (58,000 men killed in one day during the Battle of the Somme) in the pursuit of the imperial ambitions of already wealthy nations and to the advantage of such a small portion of the societies of each nation involved.

Many today are suspicious of this way of thinking about ideology (see Eagleton 1991: 33–5). Yet the recent war in Iraq *was* justified through the fabrication of a whole series of fictional scenarios that might easily be understood as ideological smokescreens (Saddam Hussein's stockpile of weapons of mass destruction, Iraq's links to al-Qaeda, and so on) and these scenarios were central to a public relations offensive across all levels of the media, including the film industry, that was successful in convincing the American public to support the war. Clearly, in this case, the ideological construction of a particular cultural imagination of war – which deployed the tried and tested strategy of exaggerating the enemy's threat and potency, as well as their cultural otherness – had a significant role in permitting the war to be waged. As such, ideology as a critical term, even deployed somewhat crudely, remains useful.

That said, it is also important to acknowledge that ideology, in this case the construction of a belligerent cultural imagination of war, is the sum of a process of struggle. One way of doing this is to use the concept of hegemony developed by Italian political theorist Antonio Gramsci (see Eagleton 1991: 112–23). This way of understanding ideology imagines a 'world view' shared by the subjects of a society within a particular time and place to be the end product of a process of struggle and contestation. According to this view ideology is not just the smokescreen behind which the state, the bourgeoisie and the military-industrial complex protect their vested interests (although it can be just that); it is the consensus view of things, the end result of a dynamic, internally-complex interaction between individuals, social groups, institutions and power structures (Eagleton 1991: 45). A particular view may dominate (that is, be hegemonic), as with the propagandist account of World War I described above, but it will have to negotiate with other views such as, in this case, those articulated by upper-class war poets, conscript novelists, trade union members and liberal women's groups, all of whom opposed the war. Eventually, through struggle, one view may supersede another, as was the case with World War I where the more critical sense of the war did, with time, become the dominant way of thinking.

Hollywood is particularly useful for tracking this dynamic process. As mentioned already, in relation to war, Hollywood's ideological and industrial role predisposes it to an articulation of the dominant ideological position. However, Hollywood's complexity – its diverse community of producers, filmmakers, distributors and exhibitors, and its socially, racially and geographically diverse audiences – ensure that Hollywood itself, the war movie genre and each individual film will remain a site of ideological struggle.

Machine dreams

Ultimately, this book aims to present a description of the cultural imagination of war in the contemporary period, especially as it is shaped by and mirrored in the Hollywood war movie. I am particularly keen to delimit the significance of the most recent cycle of war movies, those that appear from the late 1990s. This cycle is important because it gives us a glimpse of the cultural imagination of war in America at the beginning of the twenty-first century and as such allows us to question whether the cultural strategies for representing war currently at our disposal are savvy enough to allow society to make informed choices about war's role in the world in the present and in the future.

In order to get to this particular destination it is necessary to start the journey much earlier with an understanding of the development of the genre, and the precedents for representing and imagining war in earlier cycles of war movies. Hence, a considerable portion of this book is devoted to profiling and analysing the war movie as a distinct genre, and in providing orientation with regard changes in the genre over time (see Neale 1980: 51–2). A genre approach is useful in the first instance in order to provide orientation. Yet many theorists argue that Hollywood is a cinema that does not work directly with genres in a straightforward manner. Richard Maltby, for example, observes that, rather than stick religiously to one particular genre, the film industry is more likely to take an opportunist approach in which a marketable formula, bankable star, reusable set and those elements of whichever genre seems to work best within a particular moment, will be pulled together *ad hoc* to form a profitable commodity (2003: 107). According to this formula, movies may be classified, loosely speaking, as generic, but they will not be strictly beholden to generic codes and conventions. One way of describing how different elements coalesce into a group of movies with shared generic elements, rather than a monolithic genre, is to talk about 'cycles' in which distinct groups of movies represent particular, fairly localised, industrial and cultural moves.

Throughout this book I will try to strike a balance between approaching genre as mythic and structural (a kind of American collective dreaming of war displaying continuities, connections and coherence, and spanning the twentieth century) and approaching the war movie genre as a series of cycles responding opportunistically to historical and cultural change in a fierce, fast-moving capitalist marketplace. This shifting of register between genre analysis and a focus on distinct cycles of film production (as evidenced through close readings of individual films) allows the many aspects of the cultural imagination of war that have remained stable through the course of the twentieth century to be identified as well as remaining sensitive to contemporary formulations. In order to be concise and to provide a useful starting point for those new to the subject, this genre history remains partial and heavily reliant on a synthesis of the most accessible scholarship relating to the war movie. I would encourage the reader to use the citations in the text to access this rich seam of research and thereby establish their own sense of the war movie's deep structure as well as the historical complexity of its development.

1 EARLY WAR CINEMA, 1898–1930

The primary aim of this first chapter is to unearth those component parts of the cultural imagination of war that are deep-seated in the early cinema and the propaganda campaigns of World War I. Close analysis of *Hearts of the World* (1918) indicates how the battlefields of World War I were initially described through powerful patriotic propaganda films. This is followed by an examination of one of the best-known war movies, *All Quiet on the Western Front* (1930), a film that rescripts some of the earlier propagandist sense of the war and in doing so steers the genre towards its modern form.

Early war cinema: Tearing Down the Spanish Flag

War movies joined actualities, travel films, sex movies, chase films and phantom rides as one of the main attractions of the early cinema. In this early period, filming war proper was fraught with problems. Unwieldy cameras and government suspicion of the new medium, as well as the contingencies of warfare, all made war moviemaking difficult, costly and hazardous. It proved much easier to reconstruct the action in safety far from the front line. In April 1898 two American filmmakers and entrepreneurs, J. Stuart Blackman and Albert E. Smith, did just that, using their makeshift studio on the roof of the Morse Building in downtown Manhattan to film *Tearing Down the Spanish Flag* (1898). This simple film, in which hands tear a Spanish flag from a flagpole and then run up the Stars and Stripes, is claimed by many to be the first ever war movie. Released just days after the outbreak of the Spanish-American War and with accounts of the war dominating the news, audiences would have been all too aware of the symbolism of the action as well as the significance of the film's forcefully patriotic ending. The Spanish-American war brought to an end a long period of American isolationism and marked a shift to a more expansionist foreign policy. The hands tearing down the Spanish flag are hands that audiences were asked to imagine as their own, and insomuch as audiences were willing to inhabit this position the hands became embodied, entangled with the audience's own nationalist fervour.

It did not take long for reconstructions to become more ambitious. The Edison Company used West Orange County, New Jersey to stand in for the South African *veldt* in their *Capture of a Boer Battery by the British* (1900). In another early war movie a snowy Long Island meadow served as the setting for the Biograph Company's *Battle of the Yalu* (1904), a *vignette* of the Russo-Japanese War. British filmmaker James Williamson used his back garden in Hove, Sussex to stage his *Attack on a Chinese Mission Station, Bluejackets to the Rescue* (1901), a re-enactment of a military action between British marines and Chinese guerrillas during the nationalist Boxer Rebellion. This film contains one of the earliest examples of a 'shot/reverse-shot' and cross-cuts between the missionary family under attack and a squad of marines arriving in the nick of time to rescue them. Ian Christie describes how this way of connecting two discrete but interrelated events via a simple editing technique 'involves us in the crossfire of battle, placed there in a new kind of dramatic space created by film' (1994: 98). The structure here, pulling different elements of the action into a dialectical relationship in the mind of the viewer, as well as immersing the spectator in the dramatic space of war, is an early move in the development of a specifically modern imagination of war. Viewers far away from events were drawn into war's turmoil and excitement and this archly partisan and immersive sense of combat has remained a feature of war cinema through to the present day.

These reconstructions also attempted to capture some of the sense of the general reportage of events found in popular newspapers and broadsheets. Nicknamed 'yellow journalism', this sensationalist reportage most often consisted of a blend of patriotic propaganda and more objective factual reporting, and articles would often be punctuated with lurid illustrations (the illustrations themselves often based on photographs). In emulating this popular cultural form, early war movies muddied the distinction between reality and drama, and thrived on the contradictory impulses of naturalism and high spectacle. Early on, war movies had welded together what Christine Gledhill calls 'photographic realism' and 'pictorial sensationalism' in a powerful symbiotic relationship that would give shape to the emerging genre (1987: 33).

On the one hand these early reconstructions function in an aggressively realist register; they insist on being understood as *actual* representations of war and attempt to capture a *sense* of combat through the use of cross-cutting, shot/reverse-shot, special effects and the emulation of news reportage. On the other hand, their quasi-documentary form is spiked throughout with high melodrama, last-minute rescues and individual heroics. This contradictory combination made the early war movie a central attraction of the new medium (Gunning 1990: 58).

Some of these earliy films – *German Dragoons Leaping the Hurdles* (1902), *The Charge of the Austrian Lancers* (1902) and *Kaiser Wilhelm and the Empress of Germany Reviewing Their Troops* (1902) – showed military ritual and training. These concrete demonstrations of the military apparatus, as well as the social hierarchies and political structures controlling this apparatus, can be read now as ghostly premonitions of World War I, but to audiences at the time they were no doubt consumed as dramatic spectacles of national pride, social order and imperial ambition.

Melodrama and militarism: Hearts of the World

By 1904 the American film industry – like that of Britain, France and Russia – was producing thousands of films per year on almost every conceivable subject. War remained a significant fascination and moviegoers revelled in the varied attractions of prehistoric tribal warfare, the imperial struggles of ancient Greece and Rome and the Napoleonic Wars to name but a few. Particularly popular with American audiences were wars specific to American history: *Washington at Valley Forge* (1914) and *The Battle of Gettysburg* (1914) told of the American Revolutionary War whilst *The Little Rebel* (1911), *The Battle of Shiloh* (1914) and most famously *The Birth of a Nation* (1915) were set during the American Civil War. The Indian Wars and the settlement of the Great Plains were dramatised in films such as *Private Dennis Hogan* (1914), *The Buzzard's Shadow* (1915) and *The Patriot* (1916).

These latter films signal a common point of origin shared by the war movie and the American cinema's other most persistent and influential genre, the western. These roots to the genre focusing on revolution, civil war and the move westward show violent armed struggle to be a necessary catalyst of the progressive development of the American nation. America's destiny, these films implicitly and explicitly claimed, is made manifest through war.

By 1910 America's population of 92 million included more than 32 million hyphenated Americans – first- or second-generation immigrants, many of whom retained their ties to their old countries. Of these eight million German-Americans and four million Irish-Americans instinctively leaned towards the Central Powers (Germany, Austria, Turkey) as they clashed with the Allied Powers (Great Britain, France and Russia) in the twentieth century's first world war (Tindall & Shi 2000: 1013). As a result, in 1914, as the war formed into a bloody stalemate of long-range artillery bombardments, suicidal infantry charges and intractable trench warfare, it was almost as common for American moviegoers to shout in support of the Kaiser as against him. Because of this, the process of representing World War I on screen required considerable tact.

In general film producers made movies that supported the US government's policy of neutrality towards the European warring nations. *Be Neutral* (1914) shows a heated argument among four men over the subject of neutrality. A common narrative trope, seen in films such as *Let Us Have Peace* (1915), *The Battle of Nations* (1915), *The Battle of Cupidovitch* (1916) and *Citizens All* (1916), was to show parents of families, bitterly divided in their loyalties, who are eventually reconciled through the romantic relationships of their children. These movies complemented US president Woodrow Wilson's plea that Americans remain 'neutral in thought as well as in action'. *In the Name of the Prince of Peace* (1914), *Civilisation* (1916) and *War Brides* (1916) expressed unequivocal pacifist sentiments.

In contrast to, and overlapping with, this isolationist and pacifist cycle ran a more bellicose strain. *The Battle Cry of Peace* (1915), produced and directed by J. Stuart Blackton (co-producer of *Tearing Down the Spanish Flag*), was a 'preparedness' film based on Hudson Maxim's bestselling book, *Defenseless America* (1915). Designed to inform the American public of the dangers of not being fully prepared for war the film starts with Maxim (brother of the inventor of the machine-gun and heir to the family-run munitions business) delivering a lecture about the danger America faces as an unarmed nation. The film then dramatises the invasion of America by a foreign army (marked clearly in the film as Germanic) who proceed to ransack New York. The film was released shortly after the sinking of the passenger liner *Lusitania* by a German U-boat (of the 1,198 people killed, 128 were Americans) and chimed with rising anti-German feeling. It proved a great commercial success and more preparedness films quickly followed, including *The Fall of a Nation* (1916, a play on *The Birth of a Nation*) and *Bullets and Brown Eyes* (1916), a hysterical movie that shows Germans bayoneting children and raping women. *Perkin's Peace Party* (1916) and *In Again, Out Again* (1917) showed pacifists and isolationists as foolish, misguided and tricked by enemy agents. Each of these films claimed war to be sometimes just and necessary and encouraged moviegoers to entertain the possibility that America may be required to wage war in the near future.

As these examples show, up until 1917 Hollywood's representation of the war was not singular and displayed what Leslie DeBauche labels a 'practical patriotism' (1997: 195), with Hollywood producing and releasing a raft of movies that responded opportunistically to rapidly changing events. However, as the war progressed the American government increasingly sided with the Allies, advancing them $2 billion in loans by 1917 (Germany received only $27 million) (Tindall & Shi 2000: 1014). The struggle to maintain a consensus around the policy of neutrality eventually came to an end with America's entry into the war on 6 April 1917, at which point pacifist films were immediately banned and movies showing unbridled support for the Allies, as well as the benefits of preparedness, became the dominant trend.

As one would expect, the move to a war economy coincided with a vastly increased production of war movies. Anthony Slide notes that 58 fictional features and 36 short subjects had the war as their primary subject matter in 1917, with an increase to 119 features and 28 shorts in 1918 (1994: 211). The government was quick to create a Division of Films, a component part of the Committee on Public Information (CPI), headed by George Creel. The CPI considered the cinema critical to the war effort, and especially to the process of raising funds to pay for the war. As a result, moviegoers paid a special admission tax and were bombarded with propaganda films. Cinema lobbies often became the site of money-raising Liberty Loan drives, sponsored events and personal appearances by Hollywood stars, as well as being used by Army and Navy recruitment officers to cajole people into the armed forces.

Creel sold Wilson on the idea that the best approach to influencing public opinion was 'expression, not repression', propaganda not censorship, and in pursuit of this the CPI encouraged and sanctioned a particularly vociferous cycle of anti-German propaganda films. Marking the shift from earlier ambivalence, films such as *The Little American* (1917), starring Mary Pickford (a key figure in the various Liberty Loan drives) grossly caricatured the Kaiser and his soldiers, playing in particular on the brutalisation of civilians, especially women and children. Similar tendencies appeared in *My Four Years in Germany* (1918), *Daughter of France* (1918) and *Kaiser, The Beast of Berlin* (1918). One particularly successful movie was *Womanhood, the Glory of the Nation* (1917), a reprise of the 'America invaded' narrative of *The Battle Cry of Peace* that contained numerous scenes of rape and torture, including the execution of an American Joan of Arc figure. These films were so successful in whipping up anti-German feeling that they triggered riots in some large American cities (Koppes & Black 1990: 49).

The most renowned film of this period, *Hearts of the World*, directed by D. W. Griffith, was released in March 1918, on the first day of the Third Liberty Loan drive, and was greeted by its initial Los Angeles audience with a rousing ovation. Conceptualised from the outset as a propaganda piece, the film's narrative depicts a romance between two Americans living in a rural village in France whose blossoming relationship is interrupted by the arrival of war and invading German troops. As they struggle to be together they suffer slavery, imprisonment, starvation and sexual predation. After much violence and struggle, the movie ends with the couple reunited and Allied troops liberating the village (see Merritt 1981: 49–52).

Griffith purchased real footage of the front from early documentarist Frank Kleinschmidt and deftly knitted it into the film's story of young lovers separated by war. This documentary footage contributed ready-made, epic establishing shots and also provided a portal between the cinema and the cultural imagination of the war as shaped by the newsreels (the first, *Pathé Weekly*, started in 1911). James Metcalfe, reviewing the film in *Life* (18 April 1919), noted that

Many of the war pictures shown in *Hearts of the World* were taken at the actual front and under fire of the enemy's guns. With remark-

able skills they have been woven into the warp of the play, so that
it is difficult to distinguish real scenes from the manufactured ones.
(quoted in Slide 1994: 110)

In refusing to hold fast to a separation between film representation and
actuality, *Hearts of the World* is a useful example of how the war movie
genre of the late 1910s continued the tendency of early war movies to blur
the boundary between reality and representation.

Other than this skilful entanglement of real and fictional footage, the
propagandist strategies deployed by the movie are pretty conventional and
consonant with the general pattern of rabidly anti-German sentiment found
in most World War I movies of the time. The marketing for the film consisted
of a picture of the film's central character, Marie Stephenson (Lilian Gish),
being horse-whipped by a tumescent German officer. As this marketing
image shows, the film harnessed the experience of World War I to the previously well-worked narrative and dramatic templates of nineteenth-century
popular fiction. The importance of the perceived defilement of women as a
provocation to wage war was already a well-rehearsed move, whether that
defilement came at the hands of the Southern Negro (as dramatised in
The Birth of a Nation) or the militaristic German. Either way, the imperilled
female figure comes to personify a certain sacred blend of innocence, puri-
ty and perseverance, and this personification fortifies a particular group
identity (in *The Birth of a Nation* the South, in *Hearts of the World* a more
inclusive Americanism) and demands its staunch defence.

Studiously avoiding any address of the historical conditions that had
led to war – Russell Merritt comments that war 'doesn't brew in *Hearts
of the World*; it explodes, whirling out of nowhere' (1981: 53) – the afore-
mentioned aspects of the movie indicate how the film's value system
rationalises war through Victorian codes of gentility and chivalry, and a
historically specific sense of honour, duty and valour. Critics at the time
of the film's release and afterwards have suggested that this value system
was singularly unsuited to describing the experience of World War I (see
Merritt 1981: 53–4). Yet, as we shall see, aspects of this thematic approach
to war, especially its representation of gender, would blend into the later
American war cinema of the 1930s and 1940s.

Although the film does use some documentary film footage, most of the
movie's battle sequences are elaborately staged reconstructions. Griffith

had visited the Western Front but announced himself to be impressed with the cinematic potential of actual war. He complained that in the trenches, 'there is nothing but filth and dirt and the most sickening smells' (quoted in Merritt 1981: 59). And he told a reporter from *Motography* (27 October 1917) that 'viewed as drama, the war is in some ways disappointing' (quoted in Slide 1994: 109). Uninterested in finding new form for the unsettling experience of the Western Front, Griffith instead retreated to California and made World War I in the image of his earlier Civil War epics. Merritt argues this as one of the film's major shortcomings:

> The idea of finding a new image of war, appropriate to the tedium of the trenches, was scrapped – or at least postponed. In its stead were panoramas and inserts adapted directly from shots in his Civil War epic. Pitched battles featuring cavalry charges, bursting smoke bombs, and running infantry; long columns of marching men; cannons bombarding the enemy; and inserts of war machinery all served to given him a modern-day equivalent of his battle of Petersberg. (1981: 52)

According to Merritt the commitment to rapidly dating ideals displayed by the film's narrative is extended out to the film's form, and especially its battle sequences, which describe war in outmoded terms.

The result of these tendencies is a movie of transition and a war cinema thriving on contradiction. *Hearts of the World* offered audiences the familiar pleasures of the cinema – the romantic scenarios and melodramatic poses – 'woven' into a more direct, immediate and, in the words of Metcalfe, 'real' sense of war garnered from the use of documentary footage. These tendencies were combined with a hysterical exaggeration of enemy atrocity and elaborately staged battle sequences. Merritt concludes that the result is

> a hodge-podge of current history, prophecy, and war spectacle mixed with a pastoral love story – an effort to enfold the lowly, anonymous newsreel in the grandeur of epic narrative. (1981: 46)

This entangled sense of war, at the same time real *and* sensational, materialist *and* melodramatic, patriotic *and* propagandist, is a usefully contingent point of departure for the description of the war cinema as it continues to take shape in the 1930s and 1940s.

War is hell: All Quiet on the Western Front

Steve Neale notes that the nature and duration of production schedules meant that over fifty war-related feature films were released in 1919, a year after the war's close (2000: 129). These movies (the tail-end of wartime film production) overlapped with a brief cycle of revenge films, including *Why Germany Must Pay* (1918), *The Heart of Humanity* (1919) and *Behind the Door* (1919), the latter a particularly shocking Thomas Ince movie in which a German-American taxidermist, whose wife has been raped and murdered by a German submarine crew, captures the captain of the U-boat and endeavours to skin him alive.

Apart from these movies, World War I largely disappeared from American cinema screens and in the early 1920s coming to terms with the devastation of the war was largely a European prerogative. In Europe the wider culture was shaped by a process of historical revision that railed against the myths, traditions and propaganda that had helped precipitate the war and that had left over nine million dead, with another 19 million wounded. In a wave of anti-war sentiment, novelists, poets and playwrights described World War I through a stark lens and their bleak, unflinching and critical accounts proved to be extremely popular. In France, Abel Gance's film *J'Accuse* (1919), in which those killed in the war come back to life and haunt the living, found filmic form for the wider sensibility. Significantly, the film was considered too controversial for US audiences and was only released in 1921 after heavy editing.

The considerable commercial success of this jaded view of the war, a view that with hindsight could find little positive to say, encouraged Hollywood to green light the production of what critics would quickly label, the 'anti-war movie', described by Thomas Doherty as 'the retrospective Great War movie ... elegiac in tone, pacifist in purpose, and cynical in perspective' (1993: 92). Successful A-pictures in this mode include *The Big Parade* (1925), *Tell It To The Marines* (1926) and *What Price Glory?* (1926). Focusing on combat in the trenches these movies garnered celebratory reviews and large profits (*The Big Parade* grossed $15 million dollars on an investment of just $245,000). These films favoured a realist aesthetic, one that distanced itself from the florid battle sequences and archly romantic melodrama of *Hearts of the World*, and committed fully to the emulation of newsreel footage and war photography. The films map military ritual with care, and weapons and tactics become sites of fascination. The experience of war is described from the soldier's point of view and as a result war becomes more fully the province of male experience, with women's role as causal agents, or motivating symbols, greatly reduced. Most significantly the experience of battle is brought to the fore as the focal point of war, its centre of meaning.

These changes are significant but these movies also display telling continuities with the war movies of the late 1910s. As Michael Isenberg argues:

> Victorian codes of honour were by no means totally rejected, its codes of valour, honour and duty often co-existing with a revisionist verisimilitude in the treatment of battle scenes and in the use of 'hardboiled' language. (quoted in Neale 2000: 128)

Traditional frames of reference were particularly marked in those movies that showed the air war such as *Wings* (1927), *The Legion of the Condemned* (1928) and *Lilac Time* (1928). These movies glorified war through their investment in the romanticised, chivalric code adopted by individual flyers (Isenberg 1981: 114–15). Yet the air war movie, with its focus on a privileged elite, increasingly gave way to the ground war movie, with its focus on the experience of the foot soldier. Films such as *The Big Parade, Corporal Kate* (1926) and *Marianne* (1929) focused on the ordinary soldier who, empowered through his democratic rights, chooses to fight and in having decided to fight through choice, fights more effectively. These movies show war erasing previous social demarcations: upper-class American protagonists befriend and learn from lower-class comrades and ineffective military leadership (associated with upper-class ineptitude) is compensated for through the hard work and commitment of the lowly infantryman. The narratives show class antagonism being overcome in order to defeat aristocratic militarist Prussia, and as a result confirm a particular brand of American liberal democracy.

This cycle of movies distances itself from the sense of war offered by *Hearts of the World* and the airwar cycle. It garners some of the critical sense of the war emanating from Europe while at the same time fielding the experience of World War I into the manufacture of a strong specifically American postwar consensus stressing the importance of democratisation and indicating the ascendancy of contemporary liberal values. In associating the war with America's most sacred and founding principles the films could not help but recuperate a positive sense of what, for most Europeans at least, remained a wholly devastating event. That war becomes a crucible for progressive change in this way might require us to question Doherty's claim that these films had a significant pacifist intent (1993: 92). Although they are critical of specific aspects of World War I – especially the class-based dynamics of European society – they do retain overall a positive conceptualisation of war as process.

These films paved the way for what is perhaps the best-known war movie of the early twentieth century, *All Quiet on the Western Front*. The film attempts a synthesis of European anti-war sensibilities and the American war movie genre and was a great critical and commercial success, quickly becoming a technical and thematic touchstone for all subsequent war movies. Told from the point of view of a sensitive young man, Paul Baumer (Lewis Ayres), the film tells the story of a group of schoolboys who volunteer to join the German army and find themselves in the trenches where they experience the full violence of the Western Front.

At the time of the film's release much was made of the exactitude and authentic detail of its *mise-en-scène*. The film's director, Lewis Milestone, had worked in the photography section of the US Army Signal Corp during the war and as a result had great familiarity with newsreel and photographic images of the front. Actors were clad in original French and German uniforms and the film also utilised army surplus tools, packs, helmets, rifles, machine-guns and even six complete artillery pieces. Interestingly, Milestone also claimed German Expressionism as a key influence, and it is the film's blend of realism (marked by the intensely authentic *mise-en-scène*) and heavy symbolism that gives it its potency.

Constructed in a very different way to the battle sequences of *Hearts of the World*, the movie demonstrates a new commitment to combat sequences that are brutal and unremitting. In *All Quiet on the Western Front* death is instant and bloody. One particularly graphic shot shows German soldiers climbing over obstacles in no man's land; after a shell explodes all that remains of one soldier are his hands, severed at the elbow and still grasping the barbed wire. Another sequence shows German troops fall under French machine-gun fire and the film describes the action by cross-cutting between the point of view of the machine-gunners and fluid tracking shots of the falling German soldiers. In this sequence the viewer is required to tack between the point of view of the soldiers firing the weapons (a position of power) and the point of view of those cut down by bullets (a position of powerlessness). Eventually, 'the battle ends in stalemate [with] each side exhausted and back in its original position' (Chambers II 1997: 19). Placed in no man's land in this way with no clear lines of identification the viewer finds it difficult to privilege one particular force with greater moral probity or agency than the other. This is a radical departure from the one-sided point of view (with sightlines and points of allegiance clearly telegraphed) found in Hollywood war movies more generally. By also showing the pointlessness of the battle – with both sides suffering equally – this technique goes some way towards describing accurately the human cost of many engagements during World War I as well as the machine-like structure of killing intrinsic to modernised warfare. This radical representational strategy is in part explained by the film's focus on German and French forces, and it is difficult to imagine Hollywood producing a similarly balanced perspective in any scenario involving American troops.

The penultimate image of the film shows Baumer's anguished face as he retracts from the war into a reverie with nature. Reaching for a butterfly in no man's land (the butterfly as a symbol marks Baumer's lost innocence) he is shot by a French sniper. It is a bleak ending that fits the tone of the rest of the movie but it is redeemed somewhat by a closing sequence in which a shot of the young men of the platoon marching past the camera is superimposed over an enormous war grave of white crosses. This 'parade of the dead' strives for pathos but inevitably it also alleviates some of the finality of the image of Baumer lying dead in the mud of no man's land. Even so, it is still far removed from the patriotic, jingoistic ending of the propaganda films made during the war.

Of course the cultural context for the war movie had changed considerably by 1930. The prosperity of 1920s America had proved short-lived with a catastrophic crash in the stock market in 1929 triggering a decade-long economic depression. Mass unemployment and poverty inevitably reinforced the grim retrospective view of World War I. At the time of the film's release, *Variety* described it as 'a harrowing, gruesome, morbid tale of war ... compelling in its realism, bigness and repulsiveness'. The *Los Angeles Herald* deemed the war scenes 'terrific in the intensity of their destructions' (quoted in Chambers II 1994: 392). Reviewers relished the film's excitements and its unflinching darkness, and the wider audience's enthusiasm for this bleak view of the war ensured the tendency would persist. By the early 1930s, even the chivalric and romantic tendencies of the air-war cycle – in films such as *Hell's Angels* (1930), *Dawn Patrol* (1930) and *The Eagle and the Hawk* (1933) – had become increasingly hard-bitten and revisionist, leading Thomas Doherty to note that 'the doom of the battle front and the gloom of the home front were the dominant shadings [of the 1930s war film] until the very eve of the Second World War' (1993: 99).

Russell Merritt compares *All Quiet on the Western Front* to Griffith's *Hearts of the World* and sees almost everything turned on its head:

> Rather than Griffith's heroic struggle, the war became known as a hideous embarrassment, a conflict senseless in its origin, pointless in its outcome, which produced a catastrophe out of all proportion to the issues at stake. Even today, our iconography is built around trench wastelands, incompetent generals, and mass slaughter – not love-struck soldiers and stoical refugees. (1981: 60)

Although the movie has been celebrated for its anti-war sensibility, in this way it has also been subject to criticism as an inadequate and myopic representation of the experience of the trenches. The movie was based on German author Erich Maria Remarque's 1928 anti-war novel of the same name. On publication the novel had caused controversy due to its focus on the mental and physical breakdown of individual soldiers and the senseless waste and interminable slaughter of the battlefield. The novel also described the profound difficulty war veterans faced when trying to articulate their experience. As John W. Chambers II notes:

> This incomprehensibility is emphasised by Remarque directly in the statements of the soldiers and the thoughts of his young protagonist and indirectly through fragmented, uncoordinated syntax and the absence of an authoritative, omniscient narrator. (1994: 378)

Somewhere in this splintered syntax Remarque had produced an allegory of the modern subject ripped apart by the catastrophic destructiveness of the war and only this splintering and fragmentation could adequately describe the modern battlefield and its effects. Unsurprisingly, Hollywood's filmic adaptation is not beholden to the novel's complex structure. The sequences already discussed and another powerful sequence, in which Paul Baumer returns from the war like a ghost to offer a class of students the gnomic advice 'it is better not to die at all', do capture something of the unsettled tone of the novel. However, this sequence excepted, the film uses a linear, chronological narrative to follow a group of young recruits from their entry into the military, through their experience of basic training, and then to the battlefront (*Jarhead* (2005) is just the most recent of an endless parade of war movies that use this strategy). In its amendment of the novel, the film pioneers one of the most common narrative structures found in the war movie genre, a narrative structure that moves from home front to war front, from innocence to experience and from boyhood to manhood. In making the experience of World War I orderly in this way, and in tying war to the foundational narratives of manhood and masculinity, the Hollywood war movie turns firmly away from the modernist representational strategies of Remarque's novel.

In concert with this orderly structure, Baumer and his comrades remain passive and naïve ciphers for the war in general. Their lack of comprehension allows the film to avoid any criticism of the German ruling classes or any identification of the social and economic causes of war. Instead the film engages only in 'vague philosophising and a sense of individual helplessness' (Chambers II 1994: 379). War is hell and nothing more. In an excellent essay, Bernd Hüppauf notes how the film adopts the position of 'the suffering soldier as a victim of war rather than exposing the structure of violence and presenting soldiers as elements of it' (1995: 111). As a result, even though most of us are well aware that modern warfare is largely a matter of scientific, industrial and economic dominance through the deployment of air power, mass armies and hi-tech communications, the cultural imagination of war hinges, in almost all its forms and especially in the war movie, on what Hüppauf describes as 'archaic images of individual suffering and heroism' that maintain as their central object 'the fighting, running, resting, eating, laughing, dying soldier' (1995: 101). For Hüppauf this contradiction (or concealment) – so common to the representation of war – can be traced back to the experience of World War I and the strategies used to comprehend this catastrophic event in films like *All Quiet on the Western Front*. Furthermore, the film's indictment of war is only made possible through the film's sole focus on German and French forces.

The suffering soldier as victim of war: *All Quiet on the Western Front* (1930)

Hollywood was not willing to commit to such a bleak interpretation of the war in any of its features showing American units in battle. The critical view of war offered by *All Quiet on the Western Front* is allowed because it defers to the more important task of contrasting the vitality of American liberal democracy with the dead end of European militarism.

By the end of the 1930s World War I movies had charted new territory, pushing towards a more visceral, blunt, unflinching and critical representation of war. Steve Neale claims that

the foundations of the [war movie] genre were laid during the course of the First World War, when the criterion of combat inherent in earlier uses of terms like 'war picture' first came to be focused on films about modern war. (2000: 127)

More critical and controversial than most war movies of the period, *All Quiet on the Western Front* is indicative of the emergent 'war picture' in a number of ways. First and foremost, war is seen from the point of view of the infantryman, a limited and limiting perspective that reduces war to often uncomprehending lived experience. Also, the construction of the German infantryman as a victim of militarism draws attention to his American counterpart as, by contrast, a civilian soldier and subject of an egalitarian society. Second, through the film's mixture of realist and expressionist *mise-en-scène* the war movie continues to activate strong associations with real historical events and contains the sense of these events through the use of fictional story structures and the affect-driven film style of an archly commercial entertainment cinema. Third, through its episodic narrative which moves from home front to front line, from innocence to experience, from civilian to soldier, the war movie shares much with more general ways of thinking about male experience, and in this respect the war movie is also always a movie about masculinity. Last, through its resolution full of pathos and yet cloaked with the redemptive moves of mourning, memory and commemoration, the war film is made central to processes of cultural memory. This is significant because the decision to wage war in the present is often dependent on the experience and memory of war in the recent past. All these elements mark the film as key to understanding the development of a specific way of thinking about, or imagining, war in the 1930s, a way of thinking that would persist into the later genre.

2   WORLD WAR TWO ON FILM, 1930–1961

Through close analysis of *Bataan* (1943), this chapter focuses on the representation of World War II in film and the ways in which films from this period have become central to the cultural imagination of war. It is particularly important to describe *in depth* the World War II combat movie because it provides a key point of orientation for the development of the wider genre. This particular moment in American history – in reality and in film – is also essential to understanding the war cinema of the late 1990s and its self-conscious return to the experience of World War II. The latter part of this chapter – through analysis of *The Steel Helmet* (1951), a war movie set during the Korean War – briefly examines the way the genre responded to the changing cultural context and battlefields of the Cold War.

Defeat and revenge: Bataan

War remained at the forefront of things throughout the 1930s; the Japanese invasion of Manchuria in 1931 and the success of General Franco in the Spanish Civil War in 1936 were the external manifestations of the rise of militarism in Asia and fascism in Europe. America, preoccupied with the problems of the Great Depression and seeing a certain strategic advantage in the mutual destruction of competing economic powers such as Germany, France and Britain, chose to retract from world affairs all the more during this period.

The American government's isolationist stance, and the continued difficulty of reconciling the ethnic allegiances and political beliefs of

Hollywood's varied audiences, resulted in an avoidance of divisive war themes in Hollywood movies of the 1930s. The only studio to openly criticise fascism in Europe was Warner Bros. who discontinued doing business with the Third Reich in 1933 and green-lighted a number of films designed to raise awareness of the dangers of Nazism (see Birdwell 1999). The other studios conducted business as usual, with Universal Pictures even agreeing to delete scenes deemed offensive to Nazi censors from *All Quiet on the Western Front*, and 'not only from the film shown in Germany but from all versions released throughout the world' (Chambers II 1997: 23). Similarly, Paramount, MGM and Twentieth Century Fox (unwilling to sacrifice the significant profits gained in overseas markets) continued to distribute films in Nazi Germany and its territories until 1940, well after the outbreak of war in Europe. Thomas Schatz notes that

> as late as 1938–39, with many overseas markets still open and isolationist sentiments at home still relatively strong, films criticising fascism or advocating US intervention in 'foreign wars' were simply not good business. (1998: 92)

This neutrality gave America (and Hollywood, with the notable exception of Warner Bros.) the best possible platform for commercial exploitation of rapidly changing European markets (Koppes & Black 1990: 21). As a result the cinema of the late 1930s echoed the indecisive and isolationist moment that had shaped film production in the years immediately preceding World War I.

However, reluctant as it may have been to wage war, increasingly far-reaching connections with the rest of the world (marked by loans, World War I debts and overseas possessions) eventually pulled the country into the turbulence of world affairs and America began to observe the wars in Europe and the Far East less and less impartially. In response to the ferocious aggression of the Japanese and Germans and the increasing threat to strategic interests, American public opinion swung in favour of the Allied cause and by 1940 the government had pledged support for measures short of war. An editor at the *Nation* summed up the national mood when he wrote, 'What the majority of American people want is to be as un-neutral as possible without getting into war' (quoted in Tindall & Shi 2000: 1177).

In pursuit of this goal America provided financial and military aid to Britain (especially through the commitments of the Lend Lease programme), as well as using its navy to escort convoys across the Atlantic. In retaliation German U-boats began attacking American shipping and American films were banned from all areas under German control. This latter change in circumstances shifted the economic equation and motivated Hollywood to cast aside its neutrality. Or, as Clayton R. Koppes and Gregory Black put it, in 1941, 'Hollywood took its gloves off' (1990: 34).

During this moment of initial commitment to war distinct identifiable war movies were not common. Yet Schatz notes that 'war themes' were beginning to be stitched into the fabric of almost all Hollywood movies, and generally in favour of the Allied cause (1998: 94). Lowell Mellett, a presidential aide who handled liaison with the media, reported that by March 1941, 'practically everything being shown on the screen from newsreel to fiction that touches on our national purpose is of the right sort' (quoted in Koppes & Black 1990: 36).

Readying Americans for war first of all required considerable ideological work to be effected on the somewhat critical and qualified sense of war established by World War I movies such as *All Quiet on the Western Front*. In *The Fighting 69th* (one of Warner Bros.' biggest hits in 1940) World War I is reanimated, its aims clarified and renewed and its soldiers given fresh purpose. Jerry Plunkett (James Cagney) is an arrogant fresh army recruit from Brooklyn whose cowardice in the trenches has resulted in the deaths of several of his comrades. Awaiting court-martial he is counselled by a priest and as he reflects on his wasted life – and the possibilities of atonement – an enemy bombardment provides him the opportunity to escape. With all his options open Plunkett chooses to rejoin his outfit on the front line where he behaves heroically under fire, finally giving his life to save a comrade. Plunkett's conversion to the cause through heroic, selfless action marks *The Fighting 69th* as an early example of the powerful narrative trope of self-sacrifice, a trope that would figure the war movie genre through the whole of World War II.

A similar dramatic arc shapes *Sergeant York* (the top box-office hit of 1941). Directed by Howard Hawks and starring Gary Cooper, the movie is a biopic of real-life World War I hero, Alvin York, who won the Congressional Medal of Honour for single-handedly killing 23 Germans and capturing a further 132 during an Allied assault. The film shows York's transition from alcoholic adolescent to devout Christian pacifist and his later conversion to the cause of war as he decides to join the army and fight in the trenches. York is represented as a humble, self-reliant, God-fearing man, who decides to fight for his country only after great deliberation. Koppes and Black describe how *Sergeant York* 'capped an evolution in American motion pictures that took them from being fearful of political subjects to being aggressively interventionist' (1990: 39). Schatz labels these movies 'conversion narratives' and their message on the eve of World War II is clear enough (1998: 96). The conversion narrative moves its characters, and in some way its audiences, from a position of selfish neutrality to an appreciation of the need for selfless sacrifice – thereby readying America for war and steering the national characteristic of individualism towards the more collective ideal of individual rights and responsibilities.

Another popular strand of war-related movies during this time was the training picture. Schatz notes how this cycle of films overtly celebrated military technology and the Allies superior know how, and tracked the well-worn groove of the conversion narrative by tracing

> the fate of the self-assured individualist – Tyrone Power in *A Yank in the RAF* [1941], Robert Taylor in *Flight Command* [1940], Ronald Reagan in *International Squadron* [1941], and so on – who in the course of military training learns to subordinate his own interests to those of the group. (1998: 98)

With much industrial, political and ideological preparation already in place America joined the war in the immediate aftermath of the Japanese attack on Pearl Harbour in December 1941. Indicating the powerful role of war in forging consensus, *Time* magazine (15 December 1941) noted: 'The war came as a great relief, like a reverse earthquake, that in one terrible jerk shook everything disjointed, distorted, askew back into place. Japanese bombs had finally brought national unity to the US.' Doherty describes how, unified in pursuit of victory, the cinema once again became exposed to the needs of a nation at war, and 'like other industries forced to improvise under the gun, [Hollywood's] shop was retooled and its product redesigned' (1993: 4). Schatz notes that 'within six months roughly one-third of the features in production dealt directly with the war, with a much higher proportion treating the war indirectly, as a given set of social, political, and economic conditions (1998: 102). Michael E. Birdwell describes how, 'to accommodate audiences involved in wartime production, American movie theatres operated twenty-four hours a day, providing escape and moral support for a nation at war' (1999: 173).

Two powerful administrative bodies heavily regulated the production of war movies during the war. The first, a powerful watchdog organisation called the Production Code Administration (PCA), had overseen Hollywood film production since 1934. The decision to voluntarily adopt the Production Code had been driven by the need to circumvent the threat of state censorship (Hollywood did not want the inconvenience of having to tailor its products to different states, a process that would have greatly increased post-production and distribution costs) and to forestall boycotts by powerful lobby groups such as the Catholic Legion of Decency. Bound by a strict list of commandments about what might or might not be shown on screen, the PCA intervened at every level of film production and gave shape to hundreds of films that (on the surface at least) conformed to a set of rules and regulations the cultural function of which was, as Doherty notes, 'to assert moral order and vindicate lawful authority' (1993: 37).

The PCA was not a wartime body and often had an uneasy relationship with the propagandist direction Hollywood was taking (PCA head Joseph Breen, a brazen anti-Semite, officially criticised Warner Bros.' anti-fascist output in the late 1930s) (see Birdwell 1999). Still, the PCA's regulation of the economy of Hollywood movies in the 1940s did have a significant impact on the cinema of World War II. Doherty cites the example of *Casablanca* (1942) (a key preparedness film, and a conversion narrative of sorts) to indicate the frequent coincidence between the needs of the PCA and the more propagandist design of the cinema of the early 1940s. The movie opens with Rick Blaine (Humphrey Bogart) nursing a broken heart in Nazi-controlled Morocco, muttering at one point, 'I don't take risks for nobody.' By the film's end Rick's cynicism has transformed into a dedicated commitment to fighting the Nazis and he helps Czech dissidents Victor Lazlo (Paul Henreid) and Ilsa Lund Lazlo (Ingrid Bergman), his former lover, escape to America. Rick's principled behaviour conforms to PCA directives regarding the sanctity of marriage (though a cut to a revolving searchlight does give the audience, if they wish, enough leeway to imagine an adulterous sexual encounter between Rick and Ilsa) as well as steeling Americans to the war effort. Schatz notes that Rick's 'final heroics' signify 'the American conversion from neutrality to selfless sacrifice' (1998: 108).

In addition to the PCA, movies made during the war were exposed to further regulation by the government and the military (especially the War Department), as well as a bevy of newly-created wartime agencies, most notably the Office of War Information (OWI). The OWI consisted of a huge bureaucratic apparatus designed to 'gather all varied Government press and information services under one leadership' (Doherty 1993: 43). Delivering propagandist directives was considered less of a priority than attempting to shape what Koppes and Black call a 'context of interpretation' (1990: 60), in effect, a particularly favourable way of thinking about the war. The OWI pursued this goal across a broad front with a subdivision devoted to liaising with Hollywood. The movies were given particular importance by OWI director Elmer Davis, who claimed: 'The easiest way to inject a propaganda idea into most people's minds is to let it go in through the medium of an entertainment picture when they do not realise that they are being propagandised' (quoted in Koppes & Black 1990: 64).

In their definitive work on Hollywood during World War II, Koppes and Black provide some sense of the widespread reach of the OWI:

> Officials of the OWI ... issued a constantly updated manual instructing the studios in how to assist the war effort, sat in on story conferences with Hollywood's top brass, reviewed the screenplays of every major studio (except the recalcitrant Paramount), pressured the movie-makers to change scripts and even scrap pictures when they found objectionable material, and sometimes wrote dialogue for key speeches. (1990: vii–viii)

As Doherty laments, nothing so clear as a policy document or a manifesto exists for the OWI who released in-depth and constantly changing guidelines throughout the war. In general, though, the OWI stressed that war movies must show the US fighting 'against the morally repugnant ideologies of Nazism, fascism and militarism and in defense of what Roosevelt called the Four Freedoms – freedom of religion and speech, and freedom from fear and want' (Piehler 1995: 127). The OWI required Hollywood to develop a new breed of heroism premised on the abnegation of self and an appreciation of the value of cooperative enterprise. More specifically, film producers were encouraged to make movies that showed the benefits of participation in bond-purchasing schemes, actively discouraged pleasure spending, provided explanations of the Lend Lease scheme, showed appreciation of the efforts of Allies, acknowledged the contributions of women, and encouraged the unity of 'Americans All'. The OWI also required film producers to counteract Axis propaganda, especially with regard to the accusation that the war was being prosecuted for the benefit of arms manufacturers and big business (Doherty 1993: 38–44; see also Koppes & Black 1990: 66–70). With these guidelines in place, Hollywood began its move towards the production of dedicated war movies designed to meet the commandments of the PCA and the diffuse propaganda directives of the OWI. The powerful influence of the two agencies ensured that moral propriety and selfless patriotism would be central to the cycles of films produced within the war movie genre during World War II.

Circumstances made the war a difficult sell. As President Roosevelt frankly confessed, news from the Pacific was 'all bad' with the Japanese capturing numerous Allied outposts including Guam, Wake Island, the Gilbert Islands, Hong Kong, Burma and the Philippines. Setbacks in the Pacific were matched in the Atlantic as German U-boats sank nearly 400 ships in American waters by the end of 1942 (Tindall & Shi 2000: 1194).

Wake Island (1941), a Paramount 'near-A' dramatising the defeat of a marine contingent by Japanese naval forces on a remote island outpost near Hawaii captured the prevailing mood. Made with the cooperation of the Marine Corps, and endorsed by the OWI, Schatz argues that the movie 'clearly established the viability of the violent, downbeat, hyperactive combat film' (1998: 113). The movie was in production as Japanese troops attacked Wake Island and by the time of the film's release audiences would have been all too aware of the thorough and total defeat suffered by American forces, something the film's prologue makes explicit. The viewer's foreknowledge of the outcome of the battle is intended to mingle with early scenes showing tomfoolery between the two central characters, Pvt. Joe Doyle (Robert Preston) and Pvt. Aloysius K. 'Smacksie' Randall (William Bendix). This sense of premonition and the entanglement of real events and fictional characters leads Roger Manvell to argue that in comparison to the rash of over-melodramatised stories and action pictures such as *Desperate Journey* (1942), *Dangerously They Live* (1942) and *Danger in the Pacific* (1942), *Wake Island* 'achieved a reasonable degree of realism' (1974: 116).

That being said, any claim to realism is problematic and the movie also calls on the mythic resonances of earlier lost battles – Valley Forge, Custer's

Last Stand, the Alamo, The Lost Battalion – and claims (in epilogue) that in these sacred places, 'small groups of men fought savagely to the death because in dying they gave eternal life to the ideas for which they died'. As such the movie not only activates the contemporary viewer's urgent sense of the early stages of the war, it also activates a particular mythic version of American history, and this provides the audience with a 'context of interpretation' with which to order the unsettling and unpromising experience of the war unfolding in the Pacific (Koppes & Black 1990: 255–6).

The structure of *Wake Island* – its blend of specific and detailed military action contextualised within a mythic version of American history – is a useful exemplar of a strategy common to the war movie genre. According to Steve Neale, the combat movie seats its dramatic action within two narrative frameworks, 'the specific and local military conflict upon which any one film tends to focus' and 'the general and contextual narrative formed by the chronology of war' (1991: 37). In *Wake Island* the specific and local event, what Neale calls the 'initial event', is the battle for the island, while the general and contextual narrative strand situates the battle within the Pacific campaign of a world war fought on numerous fronts (the characters hear of the attack on Pearl Harbour early in the film's narrative) (Neale 1991: 36). The film appends a third framework, marked by the rhetoric of the opening credits, that situates the drama within the larger narrative of American history and myth.

The way these three frameworks are organised in *Wake Island* and in most of the war movies subsequently discussed in this book encourages the viewer to leap from the specific to the mythic. We are taken from the violent attack on Wake Island to the mythic narrative of American manifest destiny without any sense of what might be called mid-level history – Japan's Great East Asian Co-prosperity Sphere, America's lucrative partnerships with European colonial interests in Asia and so on. This leap avoids the necessity of articulating how the wider historical forces of the economy, nationalist self-interest and competing ideological systems have shaped the events under description. Quite simply, war is shown to be difficult work requiring great sacrifice at the local level, and this sacrifice is made in order to ensure the progressive advancement of American liberal democracy. Thomas Schatz claims that the World War II combat movies are inarticulate about the causes of war (precisely because they leap from the particular to the mythic in this way) and this inarticulacy can be understood as a refined structure for effecting the ideological work required to ensure support and endorsement of war and in order to deflect potential critique (1998: 106).

The film ends with the island being overrun and a coda showing marines on the march. As the credits roll, a voiceover claims: 'These marines fought a great fight, they wrote history. But this is not the end. There are other leathernecks, other fighting Americans, 140 million of them. Whose blood, and sweat, and fury, will exact a just and terrible vengeance.' The movie's focus on an isolated group of American soldiers as they fight to the death against impossible odds may seem like strange propaganda but it proved very effective as a way of acknowledging and accommodating the facts of early defeat. The film shows the coming together of the disparate elements of American society (in *Wake Island*, sternly professional Army officers, civilian contractors and enlisted men) into a unified group that voluntarily makes the ultimate sacrifice. The sacrifice encouraged audiences to feel righteous anger and to commit themselves to the pursuit of revenge. This desire for revenge resulted in unstinting support for the war demonstrated through a commitment to conformity and hard work on the home front, precisely the effect desired by the OWI.

With the financial and ideological success of *Wake Island* serving as an incentive Hollywood's output of combat films picked up considerably with pictures such as *Action in the North Atlantic* (1943), *Guadalcanal Diary* (1943), *The Immortal Sergeant* (1943) and *Sahara* (1943). The air-war movie also reappeared with *Cavalcade of Aviation* (1942), *Eagle Squadron* (1942), *Air Force* (1943), *A Guy Named Joe* (1943) and *Thirty Seconds Over Tokyo* (1943). These films relied on similar evocations of Japanese and German perfidy and heroic last stands. The films implied a continuity of process and as they were repeated in cinemas on a weekly basis fostered a realistic assessment of the difficulties faced in the war and a desire for revenge, as well as constituting and consolidating conformity and consensus around the war and its aims.

Bataan, a film typical of the mid-war cycle, displays very similar tendencies to *Wake Island*. The film opens with Japanese planes bombing and strafing a column of refugees and a hospital. Then, as Japanese forces consolidate their hold over the Philippines, a ragtag patrol are fielded together and ordered to secure a bridge as part of a rearguard action designed to allow General MacArthur to retreat from the Bataan peninsula and consolidate his forces in Corregidor. Whereas earlier conversion narratives such as

The Fighting 69th and *Sergeant York* focused the ideological work of war preparedness largely on the individual, as the war progressed emphasis shifted, and in films like *Wake Island* and *Bataan*, similar ideological work was conducted via an ensemble of characters. In this respect, as Jeanine Basinger argues, the precise and self-conscious way in which *Bataan* pieces together its patrol stands as a 'veritable paradigm' for the nature and composition of the combat unit in subsequent films, and also for the ways in which the experience of the combat unit becomes a cipher for the experience of war in general (1986: 52).

In *Bataan*'s opening sequences a clear hierarchy is established in the patrol based on competency rather than the strictures of military command. Sgt. Bill Dane (Robert Taylor) finds himself in command after Capt. Henry Lassiter (Lee Bowman) first defers to Dane's greater experience and is then killed by an enemy sniper. Dane's position as sergeant is significant as it places him halfway between the enlisted men and the officers (we learn later that Dane missed his commission by showing compassion to a man in his custody when working as a military policeman). The privileging of this middle position neatly marks the American military in accordance with OWI missives as an army of citizen soldiers, and as a strict meritocracy. These moves consolidate the way of figuring war in relation to social class developed in the 1930s World War I war movie.

With Dunn as the linchpin of the patrol the rest of the characters fall into line, each marking a carefully prescribed cultural type: Leonard Pucket (Robert Walker), a Navy musician; Pvt. Yankee Salazar (Alex Havier), a Filipino scout and Army boxing champion; Pvt. Felix Ramirez (Desi Arnaz), a Hispanic Los Angeleno with a love for jazz; Pvt. Matthew Hardy (Donald Curtis), a medic exempt from combat duties on ethical grounds; Pvt. Wesley Epps (Kenneth Spencer), a black trainee preacher from Alabama; Pvt. Matowski (Barry Nelson), a Russian from Pittsburgh; Sam Molloy (Tom Dugan), an aged cook; and Corporal Jake Feingold (Thomas Mitchell), a Jewish engineer. As they fall in, each character is mapped with real economy: a spit here, an aside there, a key piece of military uniform, and so on. By these means the patrol are shown to represent the different branches of the armed services (Army, Navy and Air Force), as well as a range of ethnicities (Filipino, Irish, Russian, black, Hispanic and Jewish) and regions (the south, the west coast, the eastern conurbations, the midwest). The various men also represent some less clearly telegraphed ideological differences

The integrated patrol: *Bataan* (1943)

especially in relation to social class (as mentioned already and shown in the different styles of leadership) and willingness to kill (the commitment of one of the men to noncombatant service). As Dane comments dryly, 'a few months ago they were all jerking sodas, or shining shoes or punching adding machines'. Appreciating the line, a script reviewer working for the OWI applauded *Bataan's* commitment to showing that 'this is a people's army, fighting a people's war (quoted in Koppes & Black 1990: 258).

Kathryn Kane notes how the narrative of the World War II combat movie invariably revolves around two axes both pointed towards the *integration* of the disparate elements of the combat unit (1988: 93). First is the narrative axis showing movement towards victory or defeat as depicted in scenes of combat. Along this axis *Bataan's* narrative is punctuated by combat sequences ranging from the random instant death meted out by a sniper, a suicide attack by a US pilot, and a long, pitched running battle. Each of these bursts of intensive action emphasises and intensifies the group dynamics, steeling the men to further acts of comradeship and bravery, welding the patrol together and undoing their differences. Presenting combat as a catalyst of cohesion in this way required careful treatment. As Doherty notes:

The War Department, the Office of War Information, and Hollywood's studio heads colluded in keeping the awful devastations of combat from the home-front screen – sometimes by outright fabrication, usually by expedient omission. (1993: 3)

In *Bataan* the body of a soldier killed with a Samurai sword remains shrouded in a sea of mist, while the body of a Filipino scout, captured and tortured, is only shown in extreme long shot. A 'safe' distance is maintained between the audience and the effects of violence on the film's characters and this strict economy of death shows death in war as inevitable, almost preordained and, crucially, as clean and quick.

Kane's second narrative axis charts 'the movement towards *integration* [of the group] as depicted in scenes of general behavior in and out of battle (1988: 93; emphasis added). The central tension in *Bataan* involves Dane and Cpl. Barney Todd (Lloyd Nolan). Todd is introduced as a lazy soldier who talks sarcastically about the war effort back home and only sullenly defers to authority. The film quickly has us suspecting that Todd (now under an assumed identity) is the prisoner who compromised Dane's early military career. Todd's questionable character is drawn nicely in a scene in which he is shot in the heel, spurring another character to note that he 'has enough to spare'. Later Dane asks him, 'How's the heel?' Todd replies deadpan, 'I'm fine Sgt., how are you?' As the narrative unfolds Todd's cynical individualism – selfish, callow, amoral and seeking to play the angles to avoid the work of war – confronts Dane's heroic team-player – selfless, professional, moral and unflinching in the face of an impossible mission. Inevitably, Dunn (never taken in by Todd) gives enough space for Todd to show his true colours and then to redeem himself, which he eventually does by fighting ferociously in battle and sacrificing his life to the cause.

Race was another key issue around which tension could accumulate. On the home front thousands of black workers moved north and west to take advantage of work in the burgeoning war industries. In doing so these workers experienced the greater freedoms of the north-eastern and western states and this inevitably put pressure on southern states to reform. This potential conflict threatened to disrupt consensus and to divert energies from the pursuit of the government's war aims. In response the OWI encouraged movies that showed America's diverse society pulling together and in particular celebrated the valuable role played by black workers as well as finding space for black soldiers in films set on the front line.

Hence, *Bataan*'s predominantly white patrol contains a black soldier, Wesley Epps (Kenneth Spencer). The presence of Epps in the patrol is explained by the chaos of the retreat in the Philippines that has led to a disintegration of the armed forces' strict policy of racial segregation (Koppes & Black note that the military 'even segregated blood plasma by race, and [permitted] German POWs ... to dine in restaurants that were off limits to black Americans (1990: 86)). The character of Epps is fairly typical of the role played by black characters in the World War II combat movie and is sketched using stereotypes common to films of the 1940s. Epps leads the platoon in prayer and sings old spirituals and through his presence and his unquestioning commitment to the Army his character attempts to reconcile some of the racial tension intrinsic to American society at the time. Doherty goes so far as to argue that the civil rights movement of the postwar period can be traced to the upheaval in racial dynamics caused by the war, not only in the changed historical circumstances of black Americans, but also in the ways in which the war cinema encouraged Americans to imagine social relations of integration, granting 'a cinematic validation – and impetus – to a civil rights revolution in the making' (1993: 5). It is an interesting thesis though it remains somewhat blind to the subordinate position given to most black characters in the war movie, with Epps no exception.

While commentators often laud the integrative tendencies of the World War II combat movie and its themes of democratic and social inclusiveness it is important to bear in mind that the construction of this particular way of imagining war was dependent on an unashamedly racist description of the enemy. As prejudicial attitudes towards cultural difference are self-consciously tackled within the American ranks, the cultural difference of America's opponents is magnified and made monstrous (Koppes & Black 1990: 60–2). On this issue Hollywood's relationship with OWI directives was often a strained one. OWI chief Nelson Poynter argued that 'properly directed hatred is of vital importance to the war effort', but the OWI wanted filmmakers to stress that the repellent ideology of the ruling elite of Japan and Germany should be the focus of hatred and not the people themselves. The OWI feared that the whole strand of B-pictures devoted to exploiting fear of espionage, infiltration and crime with titles such as *A Prisoner of Japan* (1942), *Menace of the Rising Sun* (1942), *Danger in the Pacific* (1942) and *Remember Pearl Harbor* (1942) might go too far in whipping up anti-Japanese hatred (with the repeat of the anti-German riots triggered by World War I propaganda considered a real possibility) (see Doherty 1993: 206).

Yet, as Koppes and Black argue, in an America 'steeped in racist stereotypes, and dogged by a history of virulent anti-Japanese prejudice, the temptation to cast the Japanese in racial terms was overwhelming' (1990: 250). The deep-seated racism towards the Japanese could be clearly seen in the widespread support for the government's policy of internment for Japanese-Americans even though similar treatment was not deemed necessary for German-Americans. Because anti-Japanese movies made a great deal of money for the Hollywood studios and appealed to the mass audience they were eventually condoned by the OWI and became a key feature of wartime film production (see Koppes & Black 1990: 249–77). Koppes and Black conclude that, 'In trying to soften racist imagery in the movies, the OWI was fighting not only Hollywood's racism, but a pervasive national reflex' (1990: 250).

The Hollywood A-picture proceeded with its own strategies for representing the enemy, strategies only marginally less rabid than those of the B-picture. John Dower's landmark study, *War Without Mercy: Race and Power in the Pacific War, 1941–1945* (1986), tracks the images projected onto the Japanese by the American propaganda machine. Dower notes the common use of animal imagery, especially through the association of the Japanese with apes, vermin and insects. Also,

> At a very early stage in the conflict, when the purportedly inferior Japanese swept through colonial Asia like a whirlwind and took several hundred thousand Allied prisoners, another stereotype took hold: the Japanese superman, possessed of uncanny discipline and fighting skills. Subhuman, inhuman, latter human, superhuman – all that was lacking in the perception of the Japanese enemy was a human like oneself. (1986: 9)

Koppes and Black note how 'no attempt was made to show a Japanese soldier trapped by circumstances beyond his control, or a family man who longed for home, or an officer who despised the militarists even if he supported the military campaign' (1990: 254), all redeeming features that were attributed to German characters in war movies set in the European theatre. Similarly, Doherty reads the greater presence of the flame-thrower in combat films set in the Pacific theatre as evidence of a racist mindset:

> Fire – not firepower – best suited the pestilence. The searing pain and cleansing scourge of the flame-thrower was a resonant method of eradication. Incinerated in pillboxes, fried in caves, and shot down with cold-blooded deliberation, the Japanese soldier was exterminated with a grim determination not even the supercilious Nazis inspired. (1993: 135)

In *Bataan* the enemy is not shown until the final part of the film; instead the Japanese are associated with the jungle – they are shown to be dangerous and reptilian, killing by stealth and subterfuge. They use torture and mutilation and unthinkingly obey orders. When they are filmed their faces are masks, fanatical and driven. They are referred variously as 'Japs', 'nips', 'monkeys', 'slant-eyed devils' and 'chimps'. The final scene shows Dunn, the last surviving member of the patrol, dig his own grave, and use this as a machine-gun emplacement to repulse a Japanese attack. His

Last man standing: *Bataan* (1943)

dogged killing of waves of advancing Japanese soldiers stands as a potent symbol of how the myth of an integrated American society (just, moral, determined) depended on a highly-charged description of racial threat and otherness.

When tackling questions of race the World War II war movie is full of contradictions, imagining utopian solutions to homegrown racism while adopting stridently racist attitudes towards the enemy. However, the war movie does maintain a more unified approach to questions of gender. Thomas Schatz identifies how during the war, and especially in war movies,

> the individual yielded to the will and activity of the collective (the combat unit, the community, the nation, the family); and sexual coupling was suspended 'for the duration', subordinated to gender-specific war efforts that involved very different spheres of activity (and conceptions of heroic behaviour) for men and women. (1998: 109)

These different spheres of activity tended to place men on the front line and women on the home front. The combat movie focused on the work of war – training, waiting for orders, fighting the enemy – and this work was marked as a devoutly masculine province. The home front movie focused on a different kind of war effort: maintenance of home and family, loyalty, constancy, feminine probity and (with some concession to the changes brought on by the war) hard, heroic work in the various war industries. The two spheres rarely touched one another except by the ubiquitous letters from home, a staple of almost every war movie. The rare exception – such as *So Proudly We Hail* (1943), a film telling the story of army nurses stranded at Bataan in 1942 – still adhered to gender stereotypes and emphasised the exceptional circumstances of women in combat (see Koppes & Black 1990: 98–104).

As Polan notes this separation required some rearrangement of Hollywood's dominant narrative paradigm: the heterosexual romance. Films such as *Casablanca*, *Somewhere I'll Find You* (1942) and *They Were Expendable* (1945) showed the pitfalls of embarking on any kind of romance during wartime, with couples pulled apart by the disruptive forces of war. In the first scene of *Bataan* a nurse recently married to Capt. Lassiter is driven away from the action; a few minutes later Lassiter is killed by an enemy sniper. The message in these films is clear: the war requires commitment to a clear gendered segregation of responsibilities, a segregation that requires women to adopt and comply uncomplainingly with traditional gendered positions. To not do so would place American fighting men, and America itself, at risk.

This conservative impulse, given credence by the OWI, was seen as essential to the stability of American society. Women maintain an absent presence in the combat movie, appearing as lovers, co-workers, nurses and *confidantes*. Although these female characters are often only referred to tangentially their absence is marked with a great deal of self-consciousness. For example, almost all war movies, and *Bataan* is no exception, contain scenes showing GIs writing letters home to sweethearts or ogling pin-ups of Betty Grable or Veronica Lake. In these moments gender relations remain thoroughly conventional, with women signifying plenitude, constancy and the family, and appearing as icons of a comforting sense of America unchanged by war. As well as this the technology of war – airplanes, tanks, artillery pieces and machine-guns – are also often labelled with female names ensuring that the apparatus of war takes on female characteristics. These symbols of femininity compensate for the absence of women in the armed forces and ensure that masculine identities remain stable in spite of the disruptions caused by the conflict.

Gender inequality is naturalised in the war movie through the establishment of clear spheres of influence for men and women, and through the female characters' stoical acceptance of their subordinate position (even as they shouldered the burden of men's work on the home front). Furthermore, as fighting, killing and dying, are placed in a different order of magnitude to the female experience of war, male activity is given greater authority. As such, the war movie became an important tool in the arsenal of representations that attempted to maintain structurally unequal relationships between the sexes (see Renov 1988). Koppes and Black conclude:

> Perhaps the wartime public would not have accepted sharper challenges to gender roles. We will never know, for Hollywood showed little interest in breaking out of its male-dominated formulae, and the Bureau of Motion Pictures, though showing increased sensitivity to changing female roles later in the war, found the studios resisted recognising women's contributions to the war in any but conventional categories. (1990: 113)

For all its shortcomings (some of which we can only articulate with the benefit of hindsight), *Bataan* remains a valuable touchstone in understanding the wider genre. The film, as with *Wake Island*, uses a story of colossal defeat for patriotic inspiration. The patrol works towards integration and pursues their unenviable goals in a hard-bitten and dogged manner, displaying what Schatz calls, a tone of 'grim resignation and weary professionalism' (1998: 123). As Kane notes, even in films like *Bataan*,

> the films claim moral victory because, through the efforts of the integrated group, time was purchased for others to arm themselves and, inspired by the group's sacrifice, to avenge their deaths with ultimate victory. (1988: 94)

The film's ending encourages its audience to take the powerful emotions of shock, anger and the desire for revenge out of the cinema into a world that Americans were beginning to accept was defined by war. Because the characters do not survive, the impulse to exact revenge becomes embodied in the audience who must imagine vengeance effected on some future battlefield. In order for that future engagement to be successful Americans have to fully commit to the necessities of a war economy.

The OWI believed that the movie successfully embodied a model of integration working across a number of different registers to establish an ethos of 'Americans All' through which 'the long-standing wars at home over class, ethnicity, religion and race were negotiated, curtailed and denied' (Doherty 1993: 139). Hollywood producers were quietly impressed by the film's return on investment and released a number of films made in its image. Hence, as a result of World War II combat films like *Bataan*, we see the emergence of a cultural imagination of war predicated on a powerful sense of an integrated America constructed as victim that perceives military action to be a just and necessary response to unwarranted aggression. As we shall see in later chapters of this book this way of imagining war would remain a key feature of the genre in the latter part of the twentieth century.

The genre continued to shift and evolve as the war progressed. Where the action in *Bataan* had remained firmly anchored to its studio setting (when Japanese planes attack the patrol we only see the reaction shots of the men and not the planes) it became increasingly common in films like *Guadalcanal Diary*, *Thirty Seconds Over Tokyo* and *The Story of GI Joe* (1945) for the dramatic action to be cut together with documentary footage. There are a number of reasons for this. First and foremost, the film industry (a priority industry but not one deemed essential to the war effort) had been scaled down and its personnel mobilised, and under these conditions large battle scenes were not financially viable. The use of documentary footage allowed war scenarios to be represented while at the same time keeping costs down (Basinger 1986: 124).

Another impulse driving the decision to use library footage was the attempt to tap into a new sense of war, a sense gathered by film audiences from a burgeoning mass media. As the economy scaled up to full war footing the size and reach of this mass media increased exponentially; newspapers and radio broadcasts remained popular ways of receiving news but they now competed with the proliferating images of the newsreel. The OWI spent more than $50 million per year on documentaries such as *December 7th, Memphis Belle, The Battle of Midway* (1942), *Report From the Aleutians* (1943), *The Fighting Lady* (1944), *Thunderbolt* (1945), *The Battle of San Pietro* (1945) and the *Why We Fight* series (1943–45). These films, often made by successful Hollywood directors, including Frank Capra, John Huston, John Ford and William Wyler, were heavily influenced by the codes and conventions of Hollywood filmmaking, ensuring a continued symbiosis of fiction and nonfiction filmmaking in relation to war. Increasingly familiar with the look of these documentaries, as well as the photojournalism appearing in magazines such as *Life*, Hollywood audiences began to have a particular expectation regarding the 'look' of warfare and to satisfy this expectation Hollywood committed itself to a form of realism that relied on extensive use of combat footage as well as the emulation of a particular documentary film style.

Trying to capture a sense of this hybridised film style, as well as the experience of the cinemagoer who would see newsreel, documentary and feature films alongside one another, Lewis Jacobs describes the war movie genre during World War II as 'a vast serialisation' of the American and Allied war effort (quoted in Schatz 1998: 90). This phrase captures the sense of the cultural imagination of war stretching from newsreel to feature film and back again – each individual representation just one small move in a vast mapping and endorsement of the Allied war effort and the experience of war more generally.

As the war progressed the combat movie maintained and in some cases increased its commitment to grim representations of costly, and often unsuccessful, battles. Jeanine Basinger notes how even as 'American forces began winning the war, our films grew even darker' (1986: 133). In a fascinating study of wartime censorship George Roeder offers an explanation. He argues that even though the war situation was improving militarily – by 1943 the Red Army had retaken Stalingrad and the Allies had taken control of North Africa – the need for propagandist work on the home front was as crucial as it had been in the early 1940s:

> By early 1943, an OWI memo warned that the public was getting the impression that 'soldiers fight, that some of them get hurt and ride smiling in aerial ambulances, but that none of them get badly shot or spill any blood'. It advised that the government release harsher pictures ... Such pictures 'would have a powerful impact on the sources of strikes and absenteeism'. (1993: 136)

Consequently the OWI demanded that Hollywood 'vividly portray the dangers, horrors and grimness of war' and in keeping with the new policy *Guadalcanal Diary* broke the taboo of showing dead GIs by 'incorporat[ing] documentary footage of tides washing over the bodies of dead Americans' (1993: 22). By 1946, the narrative structure and thematic elements of *Wake Island* and *Bataan*, as well as the graphic war cinema of 1943 onwards, had been repeated and refined in a large number of combat movies, including *They Were Expendable* and *Objective Burma* (1945). Koppes and Black celebrate the bleak, grim portrayal of war in *The Story of GI Joe* as the closest the World War II war movie gets to conveying some sense of the actual cost of the war on those who fought it (1990: 304–7).

By the war's close, the size and shape of the genre was significant and its borders and boundaries porous. Russell Earl Shain notes that 'during the sustained peak in Hollywood's war-related output from 1942 to 1944, one-fourth of all features (312 of 1,286 releases) dealt with the war' (1976: 31). Dorothy B. Jones of the OWI's Film Reviewing and Analysis Section found that '28 per cent of Hollywood's total output from 1942–1944 [376 of 1,313 releases in her sample] were war-related' (quoted in Schatz 1998: 102). The war-related film's box-office currency peaked in 1944, when they comprised eleven of the nineteen releases returning three million dollars or more. For the entire wartime period, 'a remarkable 32 of the 71 $3million returning releases were war-related – including ten musicals, nine combat films, and six home-front comedies or dramas' (Schatz 1998: 103). Doherty describes how, by 1945, the war movie had become 'a popular and prestigious art, a respected and cultivated business, an acknowledged and powerful weapon of war' (1993: 14).

Koppes and Black indicate how, for all its grim realism and anti-war histrionics, the World War II combat movie ultimately showed war as character-forming, essential and progressive:

> In the OWI/Hollywood vision, war produced unity. Labor and capital buried their differences for a greater cause; class, ethnic and racial divisions evaporated in the foxholes and on the assembly line; even estranged family members were reconciled through the agency of war. These images, which conveyed more a hope than a reality, implicitly argued that war, however horrible, might be a tonic. (1990: 325)

With a positive formulation of war at its heart the World War II combat movie quickly became, as Basinger argues, paradigmatic:

> The World War II combat genre existed for the period of the war, but by virtue of its popularity has remained a genre (or accepted story pattern for films) until the present day. Furthermore, once established, the combat film influenced the entire concept of the war film. (1986: 9)

Cynicism and conformity: The Steel Helmet

The effect of World War II on America can hardly be underestimated. The war stimulated a phenomenal increase in American productivity and brought full employment, thus laying the foundation for a new era of unprecedented prosperity. The accelerated growth of American power contrasted sharply with the devastation faced by all other world powers and left the United States economically and militarily the strongest nation on earth. The war cinema of the immediate postwar period was largely committed to a process of reckoning and reconciliation as well as a celebration of American victory and hope for the future.

The Best Years of Our Lives (1946), the biggest commercial and critical hit of the entire decade, tells the story of three returning combat veterans and confirms the desire to bring the war, as well as those who experienced it, into the fold of an economically powerful and ideologically confident America. The process of moving on from the war is shown to be difficult (as might have been expected from a war in which 300,000 American troops had been killed), but at the same time desirable and possible. As the three central protagonists hitch a ride on a military transport plane back to their hometown of Boone City, they fly over a huge compound of decommissioned warplanes. This poetic and resonant moment – a bird's eye view in which they are frail and awed by a muscular, industrialised, massively changed nation – is typical of the film's intelligent description of the men's troubled but eventually successful resettlement into their old lives. As Schatz notes, the movie underscores 'the desire of the studios and exhibitors – and audiences as well, apparently – to put the war behind them and to get on with their lives in the prosperous postwar era' (1998: 91).

Another cycle of war movies including *Back to Bataan* (1945), *A Walk in the Sun* (1945) and *Sands of Iwo Jima* (1949) reprised the experience of the war. Publicity for *Back to Bataan*, for example, suggested theatre owners invite war veterans to performances to talk about their experiences.

Returning from the war: *The Best Years of Our Lives* (1946)

Doherty singles out *Sands of Iwo Jima* as the archetypal postwar World War II film. The movie follows the by now familiar formula; a rifle company recovering from the aftermath of the battle of Guadalcanal are bolstered with new recruits, sent for training in New Zealand, and then thrown into battle at Tarawa and Iwo Jima. The battle sequences utilise gripping documentary footage and punctuate a narrative that explores tensions in the group as they throw themselves into the work of war and finally learn to work together as an integrated whole.

The ending of the movie is particular resonant. Following hellish scenes on Iwo Jima with flame-throwing tanks creating an inferno of battle, a reconnaissance patrol goes up the mountain to raise a flag. As the patrol clears the mountaintop Sgt. Stryker (John Wayne), the fulcrum of the patrol, is killed. His comrades discover a letter to his estranged son and as they read the letter the American flag is raised. The letter is significant because it consolidates the patriarchal force fields that have resonated in the movie, establishing a strong sense of inheritance as the younger generation shoulder the burden of responsibility from those killed in the war.

The flag-raising is a re-enactment of Joe Rosenthal's famous news photograph of US Marines raising the Stars and Stripes on Mount Suribachi.

Raising the Stars and Stripes: *Sands of Iwo Jima* (1949)

When the flag-raising photograph first appeared in the *New York Times* on 25 February 1945 it signified both victory and the still incomplete attainment of that victory. Later that same year the photograph illustrated the official poster of the 7th War Loan bond drive (with the line 'Now all together'). Part of the reason the photograph was so crucial to the wider propaganda campaign was that the men who had actually raised the flag included a Native-American, a Texan, a Kentucky mountaineer, a French-Canadian and a Czech-American (*Sands of Iwo Jima* features the original flag-raisers in cameo roles). Through their ethnic, regional and social differences, these men echoed the careful balance of differences that had shaped the World War II combat movie. The film's ending synthesises this sense of the photograph as an image of integration, victory and masculine capability with the pathos of Stryker's letter home. This synthesis produces a powerful narrative resolution that celebrates victory in World War II as well as symbolising the pride Americans now felt as citizens of the world's newest superpower. As the men walk into the smoke of battle the film closes with the words, 'Saddle up, let's get back in the war.' This tough one-liner is something of a premonition and indicates the ideological and military work that will be involved in the building and maintenance of an American twentieth century. It is a binding moment, and one to which the war cinema of the 1990s would subsequently return.

Significant fallout from the war remained. The aggressive assertion of a Stalinist sphere of influence in eastern Europe and the rise of communist anti-colonial movements in Asia prompted America into numerous political and military commitments designed to stabilise western European colonial interests and keep communism in check. During the war, and with Stalin a key ally in the fight against Nazi Germany, Hollywood had produced a number of pro-Soviet war movies, including *Mission to Moscow* (1943), *Song of Russia* (1943) and *The North Star* (1943). It was also common for the World War II combat patrol to include someone of Russian or Eastern European descent (*Bataan*'s Pvt. Matowski just one of many loyal Russian compatriots). Things began to change as the Cold War heated up and the OWI's commitment to Allied solidarity quickly gave way to a powerful culture of anti-communism.

Hollywood came under the scrutiny of the House UnAmerican Activities Committee (HUAC). Formed in 1946 to investigate suspected threats of subversion, the committee had by the early 1950s become a powerful arena for McCarthy's anticommunist witch-hunts. Among the first nineteen Hollywood figures subpoenaed to appear before HUAC accused of communist subversion were Howard Koch, who had written *Mission to Moscow*, and Lewis Milestone, the director of *All Quiet on the Western Front* and *The North Star*. Pressure of this sort ensured a glut of movies, such as *Iron Curtain* (1947), *Guilty of Treason* (1949) and *The Big Lift* (1950) that described the Cold War in simplistic binary terms as a struggle between totalitarianism and democracy. Cold War anti-communism went as far as to put a positive spin on the use of atomic weapons with *Above and Beyond* (1952) valorising the life of Colonel Paul Tibbets, the pilot who flew the airplane that dropped the bomb on Hiroshima.

Within this context the outbreak of war in Korea appeared to confirm fears of communist expansion. The facts of the war were grim: North Korean troops invaded South Korea in June 1950 leading to a UN resolution to reverse the invasion. After early bitter fighting, US-led UN forces made headway and recaptured Seoul in September 1950 before pressing north in an attempt to unify the country. At this point China entered the war and significantly tipped the strategic scales, forcing UN forces into a series of costly retreats. The situation eventually stabilised back on the 38th parallel with heavy fighting continuing until 1953, and with the border in dispute up until the present day. The war cost the US more than 33,000 battle deaths, with South Korean casualties estimated at 1 million, and North Korean casualties estimated at 1.5 million (Cumings 1988: 200). The war provided a grim 'counterpoint to the patriotic memories of World War II, challenged the easy existence of the immediate postwar years, and [symbolised for many] the death of the dream of peace in our time' (Edwards 1997: 45).

During this time Hollywood showed a renewed interest in World War II combat films and also produced a Korean War variation in which the generic template of the World War II combat movie was appropriated and applied to the war in Korea. Basinger argues that the Korean War cycle is an extension of the World War II combat movie, describing the genre as complicated and augmented by the experience of the Korean War but not dramatically changed by it. However, it might be more accurate to identify two interleaved tendencies – *cynicism* and *conformity* – that take the genre in new directions as it responds to a climate of anti-communism and to the changed circumstances of bitter small-scale wars fought under the potential threat of nuclear war.

The Steel Helmet, filmed in 10 days on a budget of just $100,000 and released just six months after the beginning of the war, is consistent with many of the dedicated combat movies set in Korea including *Fixed Bayonets!* (1951), *A Yank in Korea* (1951), *Retreat, Hell!* (1952) and *The Glory Brigade* (1953). The film opens with a grim sequence in which Sgt. Zack (Gene Evans), the sole survivor of a massacre of US prisoners, crawls through a mass of dead bodies. Zack is immediately recognisable as the grizzled sergeant so common to the World War II combat movie (the film later confirms this fact) and his presence immediately calls into play the gravity and seriousness of genre films of the mid-1940s. Yet in the Korean War movie this sense of war is harnessed to a narrative of stalemate in which the certainties of the genre (and of war in general) – integration, victory, moral rectitude – are pushed almost to breaking point. Zack provides continuity, encouraging the viewer to understand the war as part of a continued struggle against militarism and fascism, now branded as totalitarianism, and yet his psychological dishevelment and profound cynicism marks a changed sense of war.

Zack moves warily through a dangerous landscape scarred by artillery fire and shrouded in fog (in *Fixed Bayonets!* a winter landscape serves a similar function). The landscape works in a more obviously metaphoric register than the World War II war movie to signify desperation and disorientation, and the narrative as a whole hinges on this feeling of being lost, surrounded and endangered. Basinger notes that this 'loss of direction is a physical equivalent for its obvious narrative meaning. There is a growing sense of futility' (1986: 178). Zack eventually stumbles across an American patrol that he reluctantly joins. However, where the World War II patrol movie such as *Bataan*, *Objective Burma* or *A Walk in the Sun* uses the fact of being lost to motivate heroic action, the Korean War movie shows how being lost leads to internecine power struggles, cowardice and disarray, thereby rephrasing recognisable narrative patterns to register stalemate, retreat and disintegration.

Steve Fore notes that

while combat films made during World War II were virtually unanimous in their support for war aims and strategies, Korean War films were more immediately and more noticeably dialogic; from film to film and even within individual films there is an implicit, ongoing

debate over the tactics, the rationale, the morality, the cost of this
new 'limited' war. (1985: 15)

In *The Steel Helmet* this debate is conducted largely around issues of identity and ideology. Where the enemy in World War II war movies was seen as
simply beneath contempt (often in avowedly racist terms) the enemy in the
Korean War cycle is seen as dangerous because of the ideas he upholds. As
a result films like *The Steel Helmet* show American troops engaging communists in argument as well as in battle. For example, the patrol captures
an English-speaking North Korean Major (Harold Fong). As black medical
corpsman Cpl. Johnson (James Edwards) dresses his wounds the Major
quizzes him as to why he chooses to fight for a country that denies him
even the most basic civil rights. 'You pay for a ticket, but you even have
to sit on the back of a bus', the Major observes. Johnson replies: 'A hundred years ago I couldn't even ride a bus, at least now I can sit in the back,
maybe in fifty years time I'll sit in the middle and someday even up front.' In
response to what the film clearly shows to be communist propaganda the
film articulates a progressive view of American history in which a slow but
ineluctable process of emancipation guarantees that individual Americans
have good reason to commit to a common cause. In a similar exchange
the Japanese-American member of the patrol (nicknamed Buddhahead)
explains how he fought for America in Europe during World War II and that
he is American first, and Japanese second (with Japan, like West Germany,
now deemed a crucial linchpin in the capitalist system, the recuperation of
the former enemy was a notable feature of the Korean War cycle). In another
sequence, what appear to be two South Korean women at prayer turn out to
be enemy infiltrators. All these moves work hard and fairly successfully to
divorce race and ideology.

Where the film takes some trouble to pinpoint ideology as the reason
for waging war, and quite cleverly sets up a series of racial tensions to
achieve this end, it extends no analytical or intellectual rigour to representing this ideology and ultimately resorts to a very crude description of the
war in which American intervention is shown as a heroic stand against a
monolithic communist threat whose chief powerbrokers are China and
Russia. Although the film shows American troops fighting North Korean
and Chinese communists there are numerous references to Russian rifles,
Russian planes and Russian ideology. Zack states bitterly at one point:

'There ain't nothing out there but rice paddies, crawling with Commies, just waiting to slap you between two big humps of rye bread and wash you down with fish eggs and vodka.' The result is a movie that avoids any proper engagement with the complexity of the situation in Korea (as much a civil war and nationalist anti-colonial struggle as a vanguard action for international communism) preferring instead to uphold the absolute conviction that the war is the result of a Stalinist conspiracy.

The soldiers in the patrol locate a strategically important observation post (a Buddhist temple) and call in an air strike on North Korean positions. Later, as the North Koreans attack the observation post, the patrol's adopted South Korean orphan named Short Round (William Chun) is killed by sniper fire. In anger Sgt Zack shoots the North Korean Major. This historically revisionist narrative move is unusual in that it does acknowledge that on occasion US troops behave in unsanctioned ways, and it was or this reason the film failed to attract military endorsement. Yet Zack's behavior is mitigated by his war weariness and he is quickly reprimanded by Lt. Driscoll (Steve Brodie) who rages, 'Just because those little rats kill our prisoners don't mean we have to do the same thing.'

In an ending that redeems earlier tensions and once again stresses integration, the protagonists affirm their commitment to the anti-communist cause by fighting to the death as North Korean troops mount a large-scale attack. The film ends with the epitaph: 'There is no end to this story', indicating the continued commitment that Americans must shoulder in order to continue to successfully prosecute the Cold War.

The cynical sense of the war demonstrated by *The Steel Helmet* continued to inform Korean War movies through the mid-1950s. *The Bridges at Toko-Ri* (1954) is summed up by Thomas Doherty as 'William Holden reluctantly flying bombing missions over Korea and winding up dead in a ditch' (1993: 279). *One Minute to Zero* (1952) shows American artillery directed at a column of civilians providing cover for communist infiltrators (the film was based on actual events). While *Pork Chop Hill* (1959) shows a grim battle over a piece of strategically unimportant territory. This sensibility also infiltrated the wider war movie genre. The World War II movies *Battleground* (1949), *The Frogmen* (1951) and *Attack!* (1956) register the changed circumstances and cynicism instilled by the experience of the war in Korea, most notably through the presentation of military leadership as incompetent and weak. *Paths of Glory* (1957), Stanley Kubrick's powerful film set in World War I, has French Col. Dax (Kirk Douglas) defending troops who are scapegoated after a failed attack. The most powerful critique of war made during this period, *Paths of Glory* is permitted unbridled critical bite because it describes a war safely in the past and focuses on the experience of the French Army. Another Korean War-themed cycle to emerge in the mid- to late-1950s – also operating with some qualification about the war and its legacies – was the prisoner-of-war film, including *Prisoner of War* (1954) *The Bamboo Prison* (1955) and *The Manchurian Candidate* (1962). These films register the complexity of the war by focusing on the role of double and triple agents and brainwashing.

However, this critical strand of war movies sat alongside a cycle of films that conformed more straightforwardly to the wider culture of anti-communism. The narratives of these films follow trajectories in which leaps of faith are required to overcome cynicism and reassert the certainties that had held together consensus during World War II. *Battle Circus* (1953) depicts the reconstitution of a disaffected officer (Humphrey Bogart) through the unflinching efforts of a fervently patriotic nurse (June Allyson). *Battle Hymn* (1957), directed by Douglas Sirk, purports to be the true story of a professional minister who atones for 'his role in the accidental bombing of an orphanage in Germany during World War II [by] taking time out between bombing raids on the North Koreans, to care for some South Korean orphans' (Edwards 1997: 59). Doherty notes that 'the tone [of these movies] is more elegiac than antagonistic, more wistful and fatalistic about the necessity of war than outraged at its existence' (1993: 279). These films indicate a powerful conformism, recuperating both the contradictions (partially) acknowledged in Fuller's movies, and a sense of war more generally. These films indicate how even though the Korean War cycle did tread towards a cynical, questioning sense of war, one that did not take for granted the hierarchies of command, the necessities of sacrifice, or the intrinsic evil of the enemy, the cycle as a whole ultimately corroborated anti-communist sensibility, appending patriotic resolutions of hard-won victory and integration to even the most hard-bitten war scenarios.

Considering the significant impact of the Korean War in policy terms – heralding big defence budgets, a national security state, the doctrine of worldwide limited containment of communism, and so on – it is remarkable that the events of the Korean War are not better known. Bruce Cumings labels the war a 'forgotten war' governed by a 'hegemony of forgetting, in

which almost everything to do with the war is buried' (1992: 146). The reasons for this are complex, but it is true to say that apart from the cycle of
movies previously described Korea slips from American cinema screens by
the late 1950s; if the Korean War exists at all in cultural memory, and in the
later war movie genre, it is as a dark, cynical undercurrent that gives shape
to the war cinema of the 1960s and 1970s as it registers another war for an
artificially divided Asian peninsula, this time in Vietnam.

Another war on the horizon

The mid-1950s saw the release of *To Hell and Back* (1955), a conventional biopic in the mould of *Sergeant York*. The film was a high-budget
Cinemascope production that told the story of Audie Murphy, the most
decorated US soldier in World War II who was credited with single-handedly killing 240 enemy soldiers. The movie is an early marker of a cycle
of films – *The Guns of Navarone* (1961), *Battle of the Bulge* (1965), *Where
Eagles Dare* (1968) – that articulate a straightforwardly patriotic version of
World War II. The most high-profile movie in this cycle is *The Longest Day*
(1962), the most expensive war film ever made. Based on Cornelius Ryan's
bestseller, the film re-enacted famous photographs and restaged the
Normandy landings. Epic in scale, the film tapped into the confident political climate emerging in the US at the beginning of the 1960s, a confidence
that could be dovetailed more easily into the experience (and mythology)
of World War II than with the complexity of the war in Korea. In contrast to
the downbeat and cynical Korean War movies of the 1950s, *The Longest Day*
provided a cinematic echo of the strident political rhetoric of Kennedy (who
made much of the fact that he had seen combat in World War II). The film
presented a vision of self-confident military effectiveness as a brave, disci-
plined, civilian army heroically defeated the Nazis. The film's mythologised
view of World War II provided a useful touchstone for the construction of a
liberal consensus around a progressive political agenda (and this ideological move is, as we shall see, echoed by the war cinema of the late 1990s).

Maintaining this consensus would prove extremely difficult, not least
because of the experience of the Vietnam War. According to Kennedy's
foreign policy, communism was set to spread through Asia like a series of
dominoes falling and the Southeast Asian peninsula (Vietnam, Laos and
Cambodia) was considered to be a crucial domino in the game. For this

reason, during the early 1950s, America had bankrolled the French reclama-
tion of colonial rule in the region. Yet even with American financial aid the
French were defeated in 1954 by the Vietminh (a communist movement led
by Ho Chi Minh) and the country partitioned at the 54th parallel pending
national elections. Committed to a pro-Western Vietnam, America prevented
elections from taking place (the expected outcome was the unification of
the country under communist rule) and through the provision of financial
aid and military advisors maintained a series of non-democratic 'friendly'
governments south of the partition until 1961. After 1961 the maintenance
of a pro-Western South Vietnam required the commitment of American
troops. These first troop deployments were made under Kennedy as a component part of the self-confident political culture of the early 1960s. The
troop deployments were phrased as part of a mission to roll out American
cultural ideals and institutions into the developing world. This anti-communist foreign policy commitment – couched in humanitarian language and
given credence by an ambitious remythologisation of World War II – would
lead America into its most difficult and traumatic war. The experience and
legacies of this war gave shape to the war cinema of the 1970s and 1980s,
an examination of which forms the basis of the following chapter.

3   HOLLYWOOD'S VIETNAM, 1961–1989

This chapter continues the chronology of the war movie and looks at how the war cinema responds to the Vietnam War. Close analyses of *Apocalypse Now* (1979), *Rambo: First Blood Part II* (1985) and *Platoon* (1986) are used to describe how the codes and conventions of the war movie genre were found inadequate to the task of describing the experience of losing a war, and thus constructed Vietnam as a uniquely traumatic historical event registered primarily through the experience of the Vietnam veteran. Furthermore, this chapter also describes how the war cinema of the 1970s and 1980s attempted to address and alleviate this trauma in order to restore American self-belief and credibility. The overarching argument of the book requires chapter three and chapter four to be read into one another, as first a traumatic disruption of a particular embedded sense of war (and its centrality to American national identity) and then as a recuperation and rescripting of this sense of war as a way of reinventing America in the late twentieth century.

The war in Vietnam

Alasdair Spark refers to the Vietnam War as a 'profusion of wars':

> an imperialist war fought by a superpower against an under-developed country, a war of revolution, a civil war, a war for national reunification, a guerrilla war, and a media war. (Quoted in Louvre & Walsh 1988: 1)

Definitions prove difficult but what is certain is that the Vietnam War was not only an extremely unequal and violent struggle on the ground (58,000 Americans killed; 4 million Vietnamese), it also deeply divided America and severely impacted on the cultural imagination of war. America's defeat by a poor third-world country proved difficult to square with the foundational myths of American national identity, myths that depended on a powerful narrative of patriotism, technological supremacy, democratic legitimacy, freedom, good versus evil, and masculine capability.

These myths became particularly difficult to sustain in the late 1960s as news broke that on 16 March 1968 two platoons of American soldiers entered My Lai-4, a subhamlet of the village of Son My about six miles northeast of Quang Ngai City, with orders to clear the area of reported Viet Cong guerrillas. With no evidence of any enemy activity in the area the soldiers nevertheless killed between 400 and 500 men, women and children. Jonathan Schell writing about the My Lai massacre in the *New Yorker* summed up the traumatic impact of this event:

> We sense that our best instincts are deserting us, and we are oppressed by a dim feeling that beneath our words and phrases, almost beneath our consciousnesses, we are quietly choking on the blood of innocents ... When others committed them, we looked on atrocities through the eyes of victims. Now we find ourselves, almost against our will, looking through the eyes of the perpetrators, and the landscape seems next to unrecognisable. (Quoted in Turner 1996: 41)

News of the massacre steeled the resolve of those protesting against the war and fuelled tensions and anxieties in American society that by the late 1960s and early 1970s had resulted in race riots, feminist protest, countercultural withdrawal, mutinies within the armed forces and political assassination (see Franklin 2000: 47–71).

By the time of the withdrawal of troops in 1973 the war had not only been lost on the ground but the American people had also lost confidence 'in their political and military leaders [and] in the moral righteousness of their nation' (Turner 1996: 9). As Fred Turner notes:

> The Vietnam War presented Americans with a dilemma: on the one hand, Americans could cling to the popular image of a pre-Vietnam,

post-World War II America – industrial giant, loyal ally, beacon of the 'free' world; on the other, they could accept the evidence of the war that for all its industrial and military might, America was no more moral than other nations – it could still start an unnecessary war, lose it, and commit numerous atrocities along the way. (1996: 14)

Historian Marilyn Young presses this 'ethical' dimension and her final interpretation is ultimately very blunt: 'The United States invaded Vietnam against [its own] stated values and ideals and did so secretly, fighting a war of immense violence in order to impose its will on another sovereign nation' (1991: ix–x). The experience of the war in Vietnam, as well as its divisiveness, persists in American cultural consciousness as a scar, a constant and permanent marker of the limits of American power and of the fragility of America's stated ideals and principles.

Subtexts of Vietnam: The Dirty Dozen

Initially the cinema turned away from the war in Vietnam. The underlying reasons for this 'repression' of the war (the political necessity of not addressing what happened) are multiform. First, the war resulted from a gradual escalation stemming from illegal covert support for the reinstatement of French colonial rule in the period following World War II. The fear of Chinese involvement, as had happened in Korea in the 1950s, ensured that Vietnam was fought as a 'limited' war. The war was further 'limited' because it was never clear to policymakers that the American people would support the war if debated openly. The limited nature of the war, as well as the lack of any clear strategy through which to attain victory, resisted Hollywood's ready-made storylines. Second, the reunification of the country under communist rule in 1975 marked America's most significant defeat in a foreign war and this bare fact was difficult to reconcile with any of the available Hollywood narrative forms, especially those established in relation to World War II and the Korean War. As Paul Kerr puts it, 'the narrative constraints of the war genre, premised upon victory, [could not] sustain or contain the fact of defeat' (1980: 68).

Combined with this short circuit of generic precedents, war movies were deemed a risky proposition at a time when Hollywood was in the doldrums, commercially speaking. Increased competition from television (covering the war on a day-to-day basis) meant that the war had saturated American popular culture, and consequently there was none of the pressure on the cinema to provide coverage, as it had done in relation to earlier wars. As the 1960s progressed America became an increasingly divided society (with the war a key issue of division) and in response to this considerable social change and division, Hollywood – a cinema of consensus, to use Richard Maltby's term (1983: 10) – struggled to unify its audience. Studio executives searched for suitable product to exploit these changed circumstances, including courting a 'youth' audience, but, initially at least, the Vietnam War was not presumed to be the answer to Hollywood's commercial woes. Compounding this, the US military were unwilling to provide their cooperation and support for films that might criticise the war, making war films an expensive and risky commercial proposition.

As a result of these factors the direct representation of Vietnam remained marginal to the war cinema of the early 1960s with only a few peripheral movies such as *China Gate* (1957), *A Yank in Viet-Nam* (1964) and *To the Shores of Hell* (1966) referring to the war. One of the earliest films to attempt a direct address of the war was *The Green Berets* (1968), a patriotic John Wayne vehicle attired in the generic clothing of the World War II combat movie. The film is a rough remake of *Sands of Iwo Jima* (another John Wayne vehicle discussed in chapter two) but the jingoistic celebration of victory and the ideological confidence that mark the resolution of that earlier film no longer seemed to make sense of the experience of war in Vietnam. In the seminal Vietnam War novel, *Dispatches* (1978), Michael Herr, captured the sense of things: 'Vietnam is awkward, everybody knows how awkward, and if people don't want to hear about it, you know they're not going to pay money to sit in the dark and have it brought up.'

Unwilling to address the Vietnam War directly Hollywood did produce a group of films that displayed a 'Vietnam subtext', especially in their apocalyptic sensibility and critique of American principles and ideals (see Kerr 1980: 67–72). This tendency could be seen in westerns such as *The Wild Bunch* (1969), *Little Big Man* (1970) and *Soldier Blue* (1970), and in movies describing World War I such as *The Blue Max* (1966) and *Darling Lili* (1970). *M*A*S*H* (1970) uses the Korean War as its setting, yet it has been read as a Vietnam War movie. Hollywood also produced a cycle of war movies intent on inverting, parodying and satirising the war movie genre. Jeanine Basinger refers to this group of films – including *The Dirty Dozen* (1967),

The Devil's Brigade (1968) and *Kelly's Heroes* (1970) – as the 'Dirty Group' cycle in which the World War II patrol movie is brought into contact with the cynical sensibilities of the late 1960s (1986: 205). All these movies can be read as an index of Vietnam's divisive effect on American society.

The Dirty Dozen, for example, begins in a military prison with a grim scene of a soldier being hanged. Maj. John Reisman (Lee Marvin) then offers the remaining American soldiers, all of whom are awaiting execution for serious crimes, a choice: to volunteer for an impossible mission or to be executed. In these early sequences there is something of the generic narrative trope of gathering the disintegrated (often cynical) patrol together, but this is an extreme-case scenario with the conventions of the genre pushed to breaking point. Tensions are more marked than in the World War II and Korean War variants and the group includes mentally unhinged, cynical and criminal-minded characters, with Archer J. Maggot (Telly Savalas), a convicted rapist with racist views, the most extreme case.

In a sequence during which Reisman receives his orders, his rebellious attitude to authority, as well as his cynical, unsentimental and hard-bodied leadership (he subordinates one soldier by knocking him unconscious), is contrasted with a portrait of Roosevelt. As US president during the Great Depression and the early part of World War II, Roosevelt's image symbolises democratic liberalism. The contrast makes it significant that Reisman's authoritarian and brutal command displays none of the liberal leanings of Roosevelt, or of, say, Dane in *Bataan*, and this in turn indicates how the imagination of war has changed. Looking back, the experience of World War II is now rephrased, with different, more brutal, aspects acknowledged and even admired. As Basinger notes, '*The Dirty Dozen* suggests that war needs evil and authoritarian attitudes to succeed' (ibid.).

The mission at the heart of *The Dirty Dozen* is to assassinate a host of German officers (clearly defined as Nazis) as they meet to discuss strategy in the late stages of the war. In the climax to the film the German officers and their wives are locked in the cellar of a chateau, gasoline is poured into the cellar and then set alight. As the Germans struggle to escape the film implicitly recalls the gas chambers of the Nazi Holocaust, and because of this the violence is contextualised loosely according to a moral system – by burning the evil Nazis the American GI criminals atone for their own sins. Although the movie's narrative does inevitably pursue integration (the Nazis are seen as deserving of their fate, Maggot is killed by his own men,

Contrasting styles of leadership: *The Dirty Dozen* (1967)

and the mission is successful) this impulse competes with other tendencies that activate significantly different readings and pleasures. The nature of the violence – pragmatically motivated and calmly executed, retributive and sadistic – is difficult to reconcile with more sanitised versions of war found in earlier war movies. It is this violent illiberal and qualified sense of war that can be read as an acknowledgement that the Vietnam War was requiring the modification of America's most powerful mythologies, with the war movie no exception.

Bringing the war back home: Apocalypse Now

The withdrawal of American troops in 1975 allowed the major studios to entertain the possibility of a more direct address of the war and the late 1970s saw the first cycle of Vietnam War movies, including *The Boys in Company C* (1977) and *Go Tell the Spartans* (1977). The lukewarm reception of these two movies contrasted dramatically with the critical acclaim and commercial success of two other movies released around the same time: *The Deer Hunter* (1978) and *Apocalypse Now* (1979). These avowedly auteurist movies were, in generic terms, strange, rambling and inchoate. Tuned to the different economic context of the New Hollywood, they blended the epic scale and huge production budget of, say, *The Longest Day*, with a cynical and critical perspective (see Krämer 2006). These movies struck a nerve, describing an insistent and neurotic journeying back to Vietnam and pioneering a new richly metaphoric language of war. Their commercial success proved particularly significant in establishing (or re-establishing) the viability of the war movie, albeit with its codes and conventions modified to register and negotiate the experience of war in Vietnam.

The first shot of *Apocalypse Now* shows a jungle tree line incinerated by napalm with The Doors' 1967 song 'The End' providing an eerie soundtrack. We then see Benjamin L. Willard (Martin Sheen), a hard-bitten Special Forces Colonel, holed up in a Saigon hotel room. In an extended sequence that uses montage and cleverly subtle sound design, we see Willard drinking heavily and suffering flashbacks; famously the blades of a ceiling fan recall the blades of a helicopter gunship, the singular icon of the Vietnam War. At one point – in a dreamlike state – Willard has a hallucination in which he sees the final scenes of the film, a premonition of events about to happen. The film seems to suggest here that images can no longer be placed into a clear spatial or temporal order and that the clear structure of the World War II combat movie, in which localised battles are clearly plotted into a mythologised American history, has long gone and in its place we find napalm fire and psychological disorientation.

We learn that Willard returned to America, but alienated from his wife and society, decided to return to Vietnam in what J. Hoberman describes as 'a restless movement back and forth in some fruitless search for closure'

Col. Willard (Martin Sheen) begins his mission: *Apocalypse Now* (1979)

(1989: 190). As such, *Apocalypse Now* is less an account of the fighting, or of the immediate experience of war, than of the obsession with Vietnam itself, and the sense of possession it continues to exercise on those who fought there. The veteran becomes the significant locus of continued anxiety about the war's legacy and by this expedient the Vietnam War is thoroughly psychologised and made open to the work of therapeutic narratives (Torry 1993). Focusing on the veteran's experience in this way represents a crucial move in recuperating American credibility. It allows the narrative to describe the veteran's quest to find some psychological order (a tangible goal) and therefore some resolution while also avoiding the historical experience of the war and American military defeat.

However, this recuperative ideological strategy is not easy to effect. Whereas in the war cinema of the 1940s and 1950s the GI's experience forms the grounds upon which 'war can be evaluated and validated, just as his sacrifice is the war's justification, the proof of its virtue' (James 1985: 42), Willard's state at the beginning of *Apocalypse Now* indicates a serious slippage. Public knowledge of the brutal methods by which the war was fought, including the Strategic Hamlet programme (a form of ethnic cleansing), free-fire zones (geographical areas where everything and everyone was considered a military target), the civilian bombing of North Vietnamese cities, chemical deforestation and especially the cold-blooded massacre of civilians at My Lai, had ensured that, for many, the GI was no longer a site of authentic, unquestionably honourable experience but instead a symbol of America's fallibility and wrong-headedness. The GI became a reflection, or embodiment of, what John Carlos Rowe calls the 'equivocal realities' of the Vietnam experience (1989: 214). Arguing along similar lines, David James notes the 'ambivalent location of the GI as simultaneously the agent and victim of imperialist politics' (1985: 42). Some of this anxiety and confusion around the figure of the Vietnam veteran was registered in films such as *Revenge Is My Destiny* (1971), *Dead of Night* (1974), *Tracks* (1976), *Taxi Driver* (1976) and *Black Sunday* (1977). These films show the veteran as embodying the traumatic experience of war and in returning home contaminating America with this experience. Even American soldiers who had served in Vietnam chose to reject the clean, propagandist image offered by the military, and instead found ways to testify to their own difficult experience, including joining the anti-war movement (Franklin 2000: 32–40 and 61–2).

Willard bears this burden of expectation at the start of *Apocalypse Now*. Given a mission to assassinate Col. Kurtz (Marlon Brando), a Special Forces commander who – through the use of unrestrained force – is now deemed to be out of control, Willard begins his journey. Kurtz represents all the transgressions America has made in its prosecution of the war and early sequences in the film show Willard seduced by the idea of Kurtz and capable of some of his single-minded callousness (Willard kills a wounded Vietnamese woman rather than let her interfere with the mission, for example). However, although the film lets loose confusion and ambivalence around the figure of Kurtz and Willard, and the Vietnam veteran more generally, it is significant that Willard goes through with his assassination of Kurtz.

Whether or not this implies some moral distinction between Kurtz and Willard has been widely debated. An early cut of the film had Willard simply becoming Kurtz and Coppola intended the final shot to show Kurtz's Montagnard guerilla army bowing down to Willard, their new leader (Ryan & Kellner 1988: 239). This ending implies continuity of a process in which America's role in Vietnam becomes more violent and more intractable. After consideration the film was released with a palliative ending in which Willard leaves the compound after killing Kurtz and calls in an air strike. We never see the air strike directly but as the closing credits roll we see the napalm fire that began the movie, and these abstract images suggest a purifying erasure of the evidence of America's fall from grace (French 2000: 81–3). It is this ending that Michael Ryan and Douglas Kellner claim makes the film 'an allegory of Vietnam that redeems the loss of war with a myth of rejuvenated male leadership' (1988: 71).

A number of further key shifts in the cultural imagination of war are notable in *Apocalypse Now*. Unlike the pared-down studio films cut with library footage that defined the war cinema of World War II and the Korean War, the Vietnam War films of the late 1970s were avowedly epic in form as well as content, entangling ambitious production values with an activation of myth and symbol. Marita Sturken notes that 'films in the late 1970s subordinated codes of realism in order to depict the war metaphorically and find its larger meanings' (1997: 88). In *Apocalypse Now* Kurtz cherishes a copy of *The Golden Bough*, a comprehensive work of comparative religion focusing on myth and ritual in different cultural contexts, and the film shows a ritual sacrifice of a cow in its closing sequences. Through the activation of myth in this way the scenes showing Willard's assassination of Kurtz describe the event as almost inevitable, part of a universal process tied to humankind's ritualisation of violence and death.

Critics have been suspicious of this tendency, arguing that by falling back on archetype and allegory in this way the film turns away from the specific political and historical discourses within which the war was debated as it unfolded in the late 1960s and early 1970s. Jeffrey Louvre and Alf Walsh comment that films like *Apocalypse Now* 'offer a collective retreat into metaphysics, the view that war is to be seen as a darkness of the soul, an ordeal of the fallen, a version of hell, an apocalypse' (1988: 12). Jim Neilson, identifying a similar tendency in written narratives of the Vietnam War, warns that 'this view of the war as unknowable reinforces an ideologically useful historical ignorance and confusion' (1998: 143). It is telling that the *Apocalypse Now Redux* version, released in 2001, includes a sequence cut from the film on its initial release in which Willard stumbles across a French plantation and engages in a long protracted discussion with its French owners about Vietnam's colonial history. Clearly, this level of historical specificity was felt to sit uncomfortably with the vague allegorical tenor of the rest of the movie.

Although Walsh and Louvre's criticisms are apposite, the activation of myth *does* work effectively as critique in a number of key sequences. For example, when Col. Kilgore's (Robert Duvall) Air Cavalry attack a Viet Cong-controlled village, the attack begins with cavalry buglers blowing *reveille* – a historical reference to the western movie genre and to the Indian Wars. The image recalls the forging of American national identity in the open spaces of the western plains, and in particular the idea of 'manifest destiny'. President Kennedy had self-consciously activated this discourse when he asked Americans to imagine Southeast Asia as a 'new frontier' upon which a new Americanism could be founded. Yet by the time of the film's release the idea of manifest destiny had undergone considerable historical revision. As a result of political consciousness raising by the anti-war and civil rights movements the experience of the Vietnamese had been brought into a comparative framework with the experience of Native-Americans; with the government and the military now understood as agents of genocidal policies. As such the bugler in *Apocalypse Now* activates a critical sense of American imperialist history, rather than a celebratory account of the settlement of the American west.

Manifest destiny and Vietnam: *Apocalypse Now* (1979)

This critique is furthered by the fact that Kilgore only agrees to attack the village so that pro-surfer Lance Johnson (Sam Bottoms) can show his long-boarding skills (Kilgore insists this is acceptable because 'Charlie don't surf'). The dialectic established between the Indian Wars and surfing (a symbol of American consumer luxury and easy living) encourages a

'Charlie don't surf': *Apocalypse Now* (1979)

preferred reading of the scene that stresses the imperialist design, egoism and barbarity informing the attack and the relationship between America and Vietnam more generally. This critical structure is also present through the decision to use Joseph Conrad's *Hearts of Darkness*, an indictment of nineteenth-century imperialism, as a source novel for the movie.

The attack itself is a masterpiece of cinematic orchestration. The kinetic action of helicopters, napalm strikes and fierce ground fire is overlaid with a complex soundtrack that uses Wagner's 'Ride of the Valkyries' and Carmine Coppola's unsettling electronic score to shape the sense of combat. The viewer is caught up in the visceral thrill of the battle, and yet is also aware of participating in it from the point of view of a quasi-fascistic American military. This balance of elements creates a structure of ambiguity – the viewer is not sure where to place themselves – and the result is a sequence functioning as critique that locates the irreverence, egoism and machismo that motivates the attack in the historical precedents of previous racist and genocidal military campaigns. This structure of ambiguity is a useful indicator of a culture wracked with doubt about how to comprehend and remember the war. (It is significant that by 2005 the troops in *Jarhead* are able to appropriate this sequence and use it to fuel their jingoistic fervour on the eve of the first Gulf War. The troops make a wilful misreading, as the film subtly emphasises, but a misreading only possible because of the ambiguity of the initial representation.)

The tensions in America in the 1960 and 1970s (partly the result of the war) had led to a search for new ways of describing war and *Apocalypse Now* is the result of this search. These new ways of describing war have their inadequacies and blindspots but they also stand as unusual moments of tension between the interests of the state and the entertainment industry, whose search for a new audience was leading it in new directions. The result is a more wide-ranging and questioning war movie that moves beyond the embedded representational strategies and foundational myths deployed by the war movie genre before Vietnam.

That said, while occasional sequences in the film are effective in critiquing the war, the overarching tendency is towards recuperation, primarily through the privileging of the experience of the Vietnam veteran. Vietnam had become an experience, thoroughly psychologised and largely a-historical, and as a result the war became more open to a therapeutic discourse put in play around the figure of the veteran. The ending of the film, previously described, indicates that Willard has maintained his moral bearings even in the metaphorical heart of darkness that the film constructs.

Further representation is required to effect his return and something of this can be seen in the Vietnam War movies released around the same time. In *Coming Home* (1978), Luke Martin (John Voight), a disabled Vietnam veteran, reclaims masculine capability by securing the love of a good woman, Sally Hyde (Jane Fonda). In *The Deer Hunter* a group of male friends from a Pennsylvanian steel town go to Vietnam and return with varying degrees of psychological and physical damage. The film's ambiguous closing sequence – in which the surviving characters mourn the death of Nicky (Christopher Walken) by singing 'God Bless America' – registers the difficult process of reconciling their experience of war but also indicates that this work is at least possible. Steve Neale claims that the cycle of Vietnam War movies from the late 1970s 'all tended to stress loss and impairment – the loss or impairment of American moral, political and military superiority as well of the lives, bodies, innocence or sanity of its troops – as fundamental hallmarks of the war and its aftermath' (2000: 132). Although Neale's description is accurate it is important to acknowledge the early stages of a more general cultural move to repair this damage. The tendency – American soldiers with damaged minds or bodies moved some way towards the healing of their traumatic experience – is glimpsed in the films of the late 1970s and it is a tendency that takes clearer shape in the 1980s as the dominant mechanism for dealing with the traumatic legacy of the war.

With the return of Vietnam to the screens a significantly revised version of World War II also appeared, including films like *Midway* (1976, the sixth-largest grossing film in the year of its release), *A Bridge Too Far* (1977), *MacArthur: The Rebel General* (1977) and *Cross of Iron* (1977). *All Quiet on the Western Front* also returned to the screen in a bleak remake (1979). Paul Edwards notes that although these movies were more conventional in nature than the dedicated Vietnam War movies, 'there was no effort to disguise the failures of military organisation' (1997: 13). The wider war movie genre had registered the experience of losing a war and although World War II remained a source of redemptive war stories even this most reassuring of wars was subject to some critical reinterpretation.

The election of Ronald Reagan in 1981 confirmed and consolidated the rise of a powerful right-wing consensus in America formulated around free market economics, family values and Christian fundamentalism. Reagan talked tough on communism and displayed a new commitment to military intervention that led to small-scale conflicts in Panama, Nicaragua, Haiti and Grenada. In contrast to the late 1970s, when America had adopted an isolationist position in relation to world affairs, the Reagan administration's increased commitment to the use of military power as a political tool required acknowledgement and revision of the experience of the Vietnam War.

Marilyn Young notes that by the early 1980s popular revulsion from the Vietnam War had been sufficiently serious so as to merit a special designation: 'the Vietnam syndrome'.

> Thus pathologised, its symptoms – grave reluctance to send American troops abroad, close questioning of administration interventionist appeals, consistent poll results indicating that an overwhelming majority judge the Vietnam War to have been not simply a mistake but fundamentally wrong – require a cure, a pacification programme. (1995: 638)

It is to this process of pacification that we see the Reagan administration turning in the 1980s, with the war being just one crucial aspect of the 1960s and 1970s – along with affirmative action, abortion law, women's rights, and so on – which required revision. Reagan capitalised on the considerable ideological work already conducted (by the films discussed above) since the war's close, ideological work that had associated the experience of the Vietnam War solely with the experience of the Vietnam veteran. In a campaign speech to the Veterans of Foreign Wars, he said:

> For too long, we have lived with the 'Vietnam Syndrome'… It is time we recognised that [in Vietnam] ours was, in truth, a noble cause … We dishonour the memory of 50,000 young Americans who died in that cause when we give way to feelings of guilt as if we were doing something shameful. (Quoted in Turner 1996: 15)

The corollary to the political rhetoric of Reagan can be located in the war cinema of the 1980s, especially in the three *Rambo* movies – *First Blood* (1982), *Rambo: First Blood Part II* (1985) and *Rambo III* (1988). Jeffrey Walsh argues that each film can be read as 'relating to and constituted by different phases of post-Vietnam American culture' (1988: 50). The *Rambo* movies are based on characters that first appeared in David Morrell's novel, *First Blood*, written in 1972. Walsh argues that Morrell's novel – through its focus on the psychologically-damaged Vietnam veteran, excessive violence, and the castigation of the insensitivity and corruption of those in power – chimed with early post-war attitudes of disillusionment. America's contradictory relationship with Vietnam is evidenced by the fact that John Rambo's multiple killings 'are presented as not entirely without justification' but also that in spite of eliciting some sympathy 'Rambo is killed off like a dangerous animal' (1988: 59).

The novel was adapted into the film, *First Blood*. In the opening sequence, Rambo (Sylvester Stallone) enters the town of Hope in search of a Vietnam buddy only to discover that the buddy has died from Agent Orange-related cancer. While in town he is harassed and beaten by the local police and this triggers flashbacks to being tortured in Vietnam. Disoriented, Rambo escapes from jail into the local woods where he is pursued by the police and National Guard. Using guerrilla tactics he evades capture before returning to destroy the town. The ensuing scenes of destruction show America and Vietnam violently infiltrating one another and, as Walsh argues, these final sequences 'clearly allude to the burning and torching of hamlets in Vietnam' (1988: 53). In contrast to the novel,

> Rambo is now differently textured, a more sympathetic hero of the new mood. His filmic representation allows the audience to identify with a persecuted veteran who has merely done his duty. Rambo, no longer inherently violent, is now a broken hero whose final weeping symbolises the United States' unconscious guilt at neglecting its veterans. (1988: 59)

Like its source novel *First Blood* displays some commitment to acknowledging the disruptiveness of the war, often in a metaphorical register of the sort exemplified by *Apocalypse Now*, yet the film also more actively pursues a reconciliatory impulse that constructs Rambo as a victim with legitimate (and manageable) complaints. Most crucially, Rambo is arrested rather than being killed, leaving open the possibility of his redemption through the work of further representation.

Masculinity in crisis: Rambo: First Blood Part II

Consequently, *Rambo: First Blood Part II*, perhaps the ultimate Reagan-ite movie, sees Rambo released from jail to participate in a mission that requires his return to Vietnam in order to get photographic evidence of American POWs. The war is now transposed into a Cold War struggle, with Vietnam simplistically described as a client state of the Soviet Union. This way of imagining war was consonant with the anti-communism stated baldly in many movies of the mid-1980s including *Firefox* (1982), *Red Dawn* (1984) and *Top Gun*. Once back in Vietnam, Rambo disobeys orders, frees the POWs and engages with the enemy, this time fighting a guerrilla war and winning (see Franklin 2000: 173–201).

In the World War II combat movie stress is placed on integration via the recognition and then erasure of racial and cultural differences within the American group. A linchpin of this group identity is a shared masculinity, the importance of which is intensified by the all-male group and confirmed through scenes of heroic behaviour in battle. Crucially, this process of integration is catalysed by the construction of the enemy in terms of absolute racial otherness. As such, in films like *Bataan*, masculine identity (blind to America's varieties of cultural difference) defined itself over and against an irreconcilable cultural difference, signified by a racist portrayal of the Japanese. In contrast, in *Rambo: First Blood Part II*, there is no group dynamic, no integration of a variety of individuals into an effective fighting force. In its place, and in line with the increased potency of the idea of the individual in Reagan's America, we have the individual as the grounds upon which war is inscribed. Like Willard in *Apocalypse Now*, Rambo is uninterested in the negotiations and compromises of collective action, which, like the high technology that encumbers him at the beginning of his mission, is shown to be a hindrance to his capabilities. Instead Rambo himself, and especially his body, bears the burden of the work of revision and ideological recuperation.

In this respect it is significant that Rambo is half Native-American and half German ('one hell of a combination', as a military commander puts it). Through his knife, headband and bow-and-arrow he signifies the Native-American, appropriating a mythologised experience that foregrounds bravery in battle, cunning, and also a vicarious sense of victimisation. Making Rambo part Native-American in this way has none of the critical effects seen

The vengeful veteran as victim: *Rambo* (1985)

in the use of this imagery in *Apocalypse Now*. Instead, the imagery constructs Rambo as a guerilla fighter (somewhat like the Viet Cong) pitched
against a militarily and technologically more powerful foe. The trope asks us
to understand Rambo as a victim fighting a heroic and just struggle against
a totalitarian regime (Soviet communism in Asia). By appropriating these
differences (Native-American and Viet Cong) Rambo erases crucial dimensions of the war, in particular America's deep-seated racist and genocidal
history and any understanding of the political motivations of the Viet Cong.
In their place is a fantasy figure of empowered victimhood defined against
the caricatured threat of a Soviet military presence in Southeast Asia.
Rambo's German lineage activates a sense of martial effectiveness and
discipline as well as ensuring a complication of any singular reading of his
position as subaltern. Rambo's outsider status also flatters Reaganism's
claim to free ordinary Americans from the restrictive shackles of the liberal
establishment, something handled metaphorically in the film as Rambo
discards his hi-tech military technology and disobeys orders designed to
sacrifice the POWs to political expediency.

Ultimately it is Rambo's hyper-masculinity that brokers the film's narrative of revision and recuperation. Susan Jeffords argues that the war movie
sits atop and orchestrates a deeper structure – the rite of passage in which

youth gives way to experience, boys become men, and masculinity itself is shaped, ordered and reinforced (see Jeffords 1989: 1–53). The gendering of war as male experience is central to the genre as a whole and can be seen clearly enough in the centrality of male experience to the narratives of all the war movies discussed in this book, as well as in the role of women as absent other. The importance of patriarchy, and in particular the inheritance of power from father to son, and from generation to generation, in films as diverse as *All Quiet on the Western Front, Sands of Iwo Jima* and *Apocalypse Now* is a clear indication of the persistence of this powerful cultural mechanism for making war comply with traditional models of social organisation and vice versa.

Jeffords goes on to claim that the relationship between masculinity and war is usually corroborative and sustaining but that the experience of the war in Vietnam short-circuits this symbiotic relationship. Early military involvement in Vietnam was described using a language and way of thinking that privileged male capability, proficiency and heroism (attributes of masculinity that remained intact even through the difficult experience of the Korean War). However, this way of thinking was severely damaged by the failure of the military (and masculinity) to impose its will in Vietnam. The experience of the war clearly demonstrated that this particular construction of masculinity and patriarchal structure of power was founded on a series of elaborate, and more importantly, unreliable, fictions. As we have seen, this crisis in masculinity is registered in representations such as *Apocalypse Now, The Deer Hunter* and *Coming Home*, which show male protagonists physically and psychologically disabled and disoriented.

In the 1980s the attempt to re-establish some kind of conventionally constructed masculinity in place of the wounded masculinity seen in the Vietnam War films of the late 1970s became central to the ideological work of Reagan and the New Right. In fact, Jeffords goes as far as to argue that this process of 'remasculinisation' is actually more important than the revision of the war's more specific historical senses (for example, America's culpability in war crimes) (1989: 53). Jeffords argues that one of the key ways in which the *Rambo* movies effect this revision is through the spectacle and capability of Stallone/Rambo's body, and that a primary pleasure on offer in the movie is the stealth, proficiency and cleverness with which Rambo kills the enemy. Jeffords notes how, as Rambo engages the Russian troops in battle, the film attributes Rambo 'godlike qualities':

Remasculinisation: *Rambo: First Blood Part II* (1985)

he can appear from nowhere, disappear into nothing, and kill
with impunity ... he cannot be controlled by the Russians, the
Vietnamese, the audience or the camera. He is pervasise, powerful
and inexhaustible. (1989: 13)

Michael Selig takes this further, arguing that as a result of this perceived
omnipotence on the part of John Rambo, the film's

fundamental ideological function [is] that of the construction of a
male super-hero, and a masculine spectator, even in the so-called
'postmodernist' chaos of Vietnam, even in the most non-heroic
character of the combat, even in the aftermath of knowledge about
My Lai and other atrocities, even in defeat. (1993: 3)

Making the same point more emphatically, Hoberman describes Rambo
as 'so phallic, he really should be called Dildo' (1989: 187). Like so many
films of the late 1970s and early 1980s (*Star Wars* (1977), *The Great Santini*
(1979) and *Ordinary People* (1980), for example), the *Rambo* cycle reas-
serts a patriarchal structure of social relations in which Col. Sam Trautman
(Richard Crenna), Rambo's former training instructor in the Green Berets,
mediates between the military command and 'his boy'. Trautman (who still
believes in duty and in America) negotiates with the apparatus of power
and fields Rambo back into military service. Re-establishing a productive

and respectful relationship with a father figure in this way is necessary because the war had caused a fracture with the past that was in some way figured as a generational schism, a break with tradition, with inheritance (Wood 1986: 172–5). Rambo and Trautman's relationship allow this schism to be closed.

The shifts in Rambo's identity from *First Blood* to *First Blood Part II* are significant of the ideological work being conducted by the films as a whole. Haunting the first movie as a drifter who has not readjusted to civilian life, Rambo signifies something of the 'equivocal realities' of the Vietnam veteran. By the time of the sequel, Rambo is brought back into the military fold and his (albeit reluctant) acceptance of his mission, his kicking against the cynical political stooges who give him his orders, and the successful rescue of the POWs goes some way towards reintegrating the Vietnam veteran back into the fold of a renewed Americanism. Rambo has internalised the traumatic experience of the war as well as having painful lived experience of the divisions within American society. However, the films show how he is able to transcend this experience and not only re-fight the war and win but also shift a corrupt government into line with his own simple, moral viewpoint. By these means the logic of Rambo synchs with the logic of Reaganism in the 1980s, both consolidating and confirming a conservative outlook and revisionist sense of the recent past.

As Rambo returns from his mission full of rage at the US government's betrayal of the POW (and the Vietnam veteran) he is asked what he wants. His reply – inarticulate and tearful – lays bare the logic of revision: 'I want what every guy who ever came over here and spilled his guts and gave everything he had wants ... for his country to love us as much as we love it.' Extending forgiveness, love and understanding to the Vietnam veteran necessarily means letting go of a political critique of the war (and the sense of the GI as a site of Vietnam's 'equivocal realities') and this cultural shift to a more sympathetic portrayal of the Vietnam veteran as victim, enhancing a tendency begun in *Apocalypse Now*, alleviates contradiction and tension. Rescripted by films such as *Rambo* (as well as *Uncommon Valor* (1983), *Missing in Action* (1984) and *Missing in Action II: The Beginning* (1985)), David James notes that 'the GI is [able to become] simultaneously (and unambiguously) a hero and a victim' (1990: 88). Walsh notes that the outcome is 'a new metaphor encoding Vietnam as a dignified struggle' (1988: 60).

Vietnam verité: Platoon

From the mid-1980s Hollywood produced a cycle of Vietnam War movies that actively resisted the cartoon-like aesthetic of the *Rambo* cycle, including *Platoon*, *Full Metal Jacket* (1987), *Hamburger Hill* (1987), *Casualties of War* (1989) and *Born on the Fourth of July* (1989). This cycle can be defined through its commitment to a powerful realist effect and the way it furthers the use of the Vietnam veteran as a focal point for negotiating the experience and memory of the war. In their careful and meticulous attention to detail, and their commitment to constructing a believable Vietnam (one often based on first-hand accounts such as Ron Kovic's autobiography *Born on the Fourth of July*), this cycle of films makes forceful claims to authentic experience, verisimilitude and historical accuracy, and gains much of its power from displacing the senses of war established in earlier films like *Apocalypse Now* and *Rambo*. Yet, as we shall see, this change in film style did not necessarily indicate a shift in overall ideological direction.

Platoon describes the experiences of college drop out and new recruit to the Army, Chris Taylor (Charlie Sheen) as he arrives in Vietnam in the late 1960s. The narrative treads fairly conventional generic territory – the platoon move through the jungles of Vietnam, often lost and disoriented, and occasionally skirmish with the enemy. In between the combat sequences the film focuses on tensions within the platoon, especially between Taylor and two sergeants, Barnes (Tom Berenger) and Elias (Willem Defoe).

The film is shot on location in the Philippines and what is immediately striking is the precise detailing of uniform, weaponry and military procedure. Albert Auster and Leonard Quart suggest that the film's greatest strength is

> its feeling of verisimilitude for the discomfort, ants, heat, and mud of the jungle and the brush: the fatigue of patrols, the boredom and sense of release of base camp, the terror of ambushes, and the chaos, and cacophony of night firefights. (1988: 132)

In the first sequence the platoon is making its way up a gully. As the troops move through the jungle a soldier falls and tumbles directly into the camera. There is no attempt to explain this collision diegetically (the platoon does not contain a cameraman) but this 'contact' between characters, jungle and film apparatus remains a quite distinctive feature of the cinematography. The 'collision' carefully emulates the look of news coverage and documentary films of the 1960s and 1970s. Documentaries such as *The Anderson Platoon* (1966) and *A Face of War* (1968) often utilised jerkily-framed footage shot in difficult and hostile environments. The re-enactment of this particular style of filmmaking (the Vietnam movie *84 Charlie Mopic* (1988) shoots the entirety of its action using this conceit) encourages the viewer to recognise the form of the movie as 'authentic', that is, it conforms to and confirms a pre-held sense of the event gleaned from television news and documentaries about the war.

The marketing campaign that preceded the movie's release had already conveyed a sense of this attention to detail by showing photographs of director Oliver Stone taken while on active duty in Vietnam, as well as advertising the fact that former US Marine Capt. Dale Dye (a key player in the construction of Hollywood's wars over the last twenty years) was hired as an advisor to put the actors working on the film through a kind of accelerated boot camp. After this 'training' Tom Berenger stated that 'we didn't have to act, we were there' (quoted in Sturken 1997: 97). Through film technique and clever publicity the film generated a field of critical opinion that noted and celebrated its realism. In *Time* magazine (26 January 1987) David Halberstam, a respected journalist and author of *The Making of a Quagmire*, described *Platoon* as 'the ultimate work of witness, something that has the authenticity of documentary ... Thirty years from now, people will think of the Vietnam War as *Platoon*.'

Yet we should be wary of the seductive nature of the film's powerful reality-effect and sensitive to the considerable ideological work that is taking place under the cover of the film's realist surface. The Vietnam War was a heavily mediated war and *Platoon* is self-conscious in its manipulation of the audience's familiarity with the event. As well as the emulation of a particular style of filmmaking – what we might call Vietnam *verité* – *Platoon* also painstakingly re-enacts a number of key photographs of the war including the burning of houses with Zippo cigarette lighters at Cam Ne, a Viet Cong suspect shot in the head during the Tet offensive, and photos of civilians murdered by US troops at My Lai. The My Lai photographs – taken by US Army photographer Ron Haeberle and published in *Time* magazine in December 1969 – are particularly well known and resonate strongly with America's often bitter and divided experience and memory of the Vietnam War.

In the 1970s these images signified a sense of traumatic defeat. Yet in *Platoon* (and other Vietnam War movies of the late 1980s such as *Hamburger Hill, Casualties of War* and *Born on the Fourth of July*) this sense of the war is reworked or to use Marita Sturken's suggestive term 're-enacted' (1997: 27–33). Sturken argues that Hollywood movies like *Platoon* deliberately restage these iconic photographs, blurring the boundaries between re-enactment and original event and establishing a more concrete historical significance than that of say *Apocalypse Now* or *Rambo*. Most significantly, this mechanism enables the film to consolidate processes of cultural revision already put in play by the cycle of Vietnam War movies released in the early 1980s. For example, the key move around which the narrative of *Platoon* turns involves the loss of control of the platoon as they search a suspect enemy village and this sequence is crucially dependent on a cultural memory of the war relating to atrocities committed by American troops. A disruptive sense of the war is activated by these sequences but as the narrative progresses we begin to see how the initial meanings of these iconic images are rescripted. Members ;of the platoon, led by Sgt. Barnes, torture and torment the inhabitants of the village. A mentally handicapped youth is beaten to death, children hiding in a bomb shelter are blown up and Barnes executes the wife of the head of the village and then threatens to murder his daughter. A soldier suggests that 'we do [murder] the lot of them'. Crucially though, the correspondence with the massacre at My Lai ends there as Sgt. Elias intervenes and in doing so motivates Taylor and a number of others to prevent the troops committing further violence. Elias also threatens to pursue a court-martial against Barnes. These sequences indicate that although Americans are capable of atrocity there are still amongst their number men who can establish the difference between right and wrong (similarly in *Casualties of War*, Eriksson (Michael J. Fox) testifies against his fellow soldiers for the rape and murder of a Vietnamese woman). Taylor, who oscillates between Elias and Barnes throughout the film, is polarised by these events in particular and in the remainder of the film adopts a stance closer to that of Elias. By this move the film redeems the trauma that My Lai (and Vietnam in general) had rent in America's sense of self.

This sequence in the film has been read as a re-enactment of the 'unrecognisable landscape' of My Lai as noted by Schell, an indictment that

Rescripting the My Lai massacre: *Platoon* (1986)

captures the true dimensions and horrors of the war. However, as we have seen, the film works to simplify and contain the unsettling experience of the My Lai massacre and to propose an alternative, less disruptive ending. Haeberle's photographs of groups of dead bodies clearly signify the incontrovertible facts of the killings at My Lai. Yet the narrative resources of *Platoon* bring the dead back to life in an attempt to find a different, less disruptive, resolution.

By its title *Platoon* displays a commitment to the generic make up of World War II patrol movies such as *Bataan*. Once again the group, as microcosm, bears the burden of representation. However, where the patrol of the World War II combat movie pursues the preferred ideological goal of integration, the platoon of the Vietnam War is divided and disintegrating. In *Platoon* base camp sees the men divide into two distinct groups. Upstairs in the bunks the soldiers variously play poker, read pornographic magazines, worship at a Roman Catholic shrine, discuss Islam and listen to Merle Haggard's 'Okie from Muskogee'. According to the logic of the film the characters – black, hispanic, white – represent what might loosely be called right-wing positions – machismo (via exaggerated heterosexuality and homophobia), fundamentalist religion, racism, sexism, authoritarianism and anti-communism. Downstairs in a bunker the rest of the platoon smoke dope and dance together to the sound of Smokey Robinson's 'Tracks of My Tears'. Once again we see black, hispanic and white characters but this time the characters are united through the collective behaviour of smoking dope and in their acknowledgement of the pointlessness of the war. This 'alternative' position offers us racial equality, pleasure (dancing, drugs, sexual freedom), collective action and rebellion against authority. The symbolic dimension here is very marked and the divide between the two groups might easily be read as a metaphor for the loose coalitions that either supported or protested the war in the 1960s and 1970s.

The narrative abstracts these two groups into the characters of Elias, a semi-mystical character cloaked in religious imagery (in the opening sequence carrying an M60 machine-gun as if carrying a cross) and Barnes, an Ahab-like character, heavily scarred, cynical and impervious to death and danger. By this mechanism the film calls the specificities of the war into play and then turns away from the trauma and contradiction at the heart of the experience and reduces Vietnam to a battle between good and evil as personified by Elias and Barnes (as in *Apocalypse Now* this mythical structure surfaces the difficulty of confronting a more properly historical sense of the war).

Much more thoroughly committed to the disintegration of the group than its World War II antecedents, the film does *eventually* commit to the integration of differences within the psychology of its central character. Taylor reconciles the opposition between Barnes and Elias by killing Barnes to avenge Elias' murder. After the killing Taylor observes, 'I felt like a son born of two fathers.' By this act Taylor sutures together the differences engendered by the war and alleviates the disruptiveness so central to the film's narrative economy.

The film ends as Taylor is evacuated by helicopter; his second wound guaranteeing the war is over for him. As he leaves the battlefield for the final time he observes that in Vietnam, 'we didn't fight the enemy, we fought ourselves, and the enemy was within us'. It is a telling line of dialogue that reduces the war into a kind of therapeutic exercise, an epiphany of war triggering personal development and growth, something enhanced by the use of Samuel Barber's elegiac 'Adagio for Strings'. What the film implies, and in effect what Vietnam has come to represent in American culture at large, is a personal ahistorical trauma that can be overcome. Michael Klein suggests that 'the film substitutes a psychological and metaphysical interpretation for a historical understanding of the genocidal aspects of the war' (1990:

25–6). As a result the film is 'unencumbered by history – by the naming particularity that would bring in its wake the guilt, shame, self-accusation and the internal divisions that the national myths function by repressing' (Louvre & Walsh 1988: 12).

A distillation of this tendency to psychologise, to remove history, can be seen in a line of recurring dialogue through which the key characters dismiss the war as 'all just politics' (the troops in *Hamburger Hill* echo the sentiment with the repeated line, 'It don't mean nothing', and the coping strategy has most recently been used by the soldiers in *Jarhead*). With these words the film avoids addressing anything seen as relating to the 'system', understood as the military, the government, or any of the political ideologies fuelling the differences upon which the war was predicated. We are encouraged to read this cynicism and willful myopia as simply a coping strategy of the combat soldier, the 'grunt' who can put up with anything. However, this coping strategy becomes a kind of solution, a way of reconciling disruptive memories of the war. Any point of contradiction – from the confused reasons for fighting the war to the racism and irrationality of the military – is squared away with the mantra – 'It's all just politics, man.' Bruce H. Franklin lists the newsletters, letter-writing campaigns, mass protests and, in extreme cases, mutinies conducted by troops in the armed forces during the Vietnam War (2000: 47–71). All these are evidence of a ferocious, committed political discussion about the war and its aims taking place within the ranks. Yet it is extremely rare to find a Vietnam War movie in which two or three GIs sit down and discuss the war in avowedly political terms. The result is a cycle of films that make, in comparison, the discussion of communist ideology in the 1950s Korean War cycle, films produced at the height of the Cold War and under the threat of HUAC persecution, seem in-depth and insightful.

From *Apocalypse Now* to *Rambo* and *Platoon* we see a number of crucial moves in the development of strategies for renewing the signifier 'war' post-Vietnam. The Vietnam War movies of the late 1970s and 1980s show war to be a serious and bloody business that divides America, yet the underlying logic of these movies drives towards a kind of redemption. Portrayed as the key victims of the war, the suffering of the Vietnam veteran diverts attention from the war's other victims (the Vietnamese) and from the reasons for fighting the war. By effacing the 'equivocal realities' that shaped American soldiers' experiences in Vietnam the war cinema turned to familiar tropes and techniques. Showing the GI displaying an insistent moral conscience that enabled them to fight compassionately and ethically, and ultimately to win if not a military victory then at least a kind of moral victory, proved a robust solution that elided cultural contradiction on a number of different levels.

David James suggests that the general tendency of the 1980s Vietnam War movie is to

> dehistoricise the war, to represent it as a transhistorical, existential catastrophe that is in essence inexplicable, unrepresentable, and itself a contradiction, and then to rewrite it as local actions, often limited military undertakings, in which the American soldiers win qualified or depleted local victories that cover for the actual defeat of the invasion as a whole. (1990: 88)

In sum, the squaring away of contradiction, the effacing of cultural and political differences, the eliding of the experience of the Vietnamese, and the remasculinisation of American male identity all make Hollywood's Vietnam war movies among the most ideologically interventionist films ever made and allow a successful process of revision to recuperate the experience of Vietnam.

Fred Turner recalls a Vietnam Veterans Against the War (VVAW) parade on 23 April 1971 made up of veterans who had been psychologically or physically wounded by the war. The parade was angry, political and resentful. By the 1990s, the type of angry and political protest march that had defined resistance to the war in the late 1960s and 1970s had become something completely different. 'Operation Rolling Thunder', a VVAW parade on 24 May 1992 treated the Vietnam War 'like other more popular wars before it … as a source of memories to be celebrated' (1996: 7). Once more, and in part due to the considerable ideological work conducted by the war cinema of the 1980s, the Vietnam War, and war in general, could be placed at the centre of American national identity as something of value, as something of which to be proud.

4   CONTEMPORARY WAR CINEMA, 1989–2006

Chapter three described how the war cinema of the 1980s – through the ideological work conducted by movies such as *Apocalypse Now*, *Rambo* and *Platoon* – recuperated the traumatic experience of the Vietnam War, echoing and feeding into a general cultural tendency of historical revision. This chapter examines those movies made in the 1990s and beyond that have combat as their subject. Made during a time of political consolidation in the centre, a correction of sorts after the rightwards pull of the Reagan years, movies such as *Saving Private Ryan*, *We Were Soldiers*, *Courage Under Fire* (1996) and *Pearl Harbor* (2001) register a shift in the cultural imagination of war. This shift sits atop a massive change in the actual way in which war is waged, a change precipitated by the end of the Cold War and the uncontested dominance of American hegemony in both political and military terms. These movies have fostered a sense of World War II as a 'just war' fought by a 'greatest generation' and this has led to a war cinema at the start of the twenty-first century that is more positive about war than at any time since the debacle in Vietnam.

No more Vietnams

In the late 1980s and early 1990s the dissolution of communism in eastern Europe and the break up of the Soviet Union triggered a series of localised conflicts in the Balkans, the Middle East and Africa. These wars – small-scale, contingent and intractable – formed the grounds upon which a new foreign policy was established. Faced with this vastly altered scene,

Republican president George Bush called for a 'New World Order' in which America would play an explicit and determinate role, if necessary through the use of American military power. Initially this policy was pragmatic and internationalist, intended to preserve and protect American interests in the face of the potentially dramatic change resulting from the breakdown of communist networks and alliances. Specific goals included regional stability in East Asia and the Middle East.

The first significant American commitment in pursuit of this New World Order was triggered when Iraq invaded Kuwait in 1990, annexing the area that had been carved from its territories by Britain in 1961. A war in the Persian Gulf followed, with Iraq's invasion of Kuwait forcibly reversed by a US-led UN force. During the war President Bush repeatedly stated there would be: 'no more Vietnams'. His rhetoric (somewhat disingenuously) insisted that America's renewed commitment to the containment of a political, religious and ideological system felt threatening to its own inter-ests, as well as the engineering of a favourable geopolitical layout of crucial raw materials such as oil, was in no way congruent with earlier imperialist foreign policies. More significantly the use of the phrase also insisted that these aims would not be derailed as they had been in Vietnam; there would be no repeat of American failure. As such the war was marked (in its choice of tactics, its rules of reporting and its rhetoric) by an undertow of memory stretching back to the experience of the war in Vietnam.

In 1991, with a combination of devastating and prolonged air attacks and a massive military offensive across a broad front America achieved the goal of pushing the Iraqi army out of Kuwait. Stopping short of a full-scale invasion of Iraq, American forces then consolidated into a holding pattern consisting of the enforcement of an economic embargo and no-fly zone and occasional bombing of Iraq's military and civilian infrastructure. This holding pattern spanned the whole of the 1990s: a clear symbol of America's complex internationalism at the end of the twentieth century, a symbol indicative of both a renewal of American confidence in its ability and willingness to wage war but also of the limits of America's power in the post-Cold War world.

Elected on a narrow margin, and with the political system in a finely balanced deadlock around the centre, President Bill Clinton inherited the war in the Gulf. In a self-conscious echo of Kennedy, and in an attempt to rebrand Bush's foreign policy as his own, Clinton argued that it was the moral responsibility of America, as the world's 'indispensable nation', to ensure stability and promote democracy on humanitarian grounds. Where Bush's New World Order had been an immediate, and fairly pragmatic, attempt to fill the vacuum created by the end of the Cold War, Clinton rephrased American foreign policy as humanitarian intervention, a reconceptualisation that, as we shall see, governed the cultural imagination of war throughout the 1990s.

Liberal perspectives: Courage Under Fire

In contrast to the 1980s, the 1990s saw very few war movies in production. The changed nature of war – small scale, localised and mired in the complex politics of ethnic conflict – failed to register cleanly enough to be figured in the limited generic language available to Hollywood film producers. Furthermore, the critique, still implicit in even the most revisionist of Vietnam War movies as well as their dedicated historical perspective (describing a war now over a decade in the past), made Vietnam an unwieldy cipher for articulating a sense of war in the present.

As a result, Hollywood's response to the Gulf War was delayed and muted. In *Courage Under Fire* Lt. Col. Nathaniel Serling (Denzel Washington), a black Army officer, attempts to overcome his feelings of guilt for his role in a 'friendly fire' incident, while at the same time conducting an investigation to determine whether or not Capt. Karen Walden (Meg Ryan), a white Army helicopter pilot and single mother, is worthy of a posthumous Congressional Medal of Honor. The film can at one level be read as a liberal 'issue' movie exploring the changed role of women in the American military (allowed partial combat status from 1994), a theme also present in *GI Jane* (1997), *Mulan* (1998) and *Small Soldiers* (1998). However, Serling's quest and his feelings of guilt, the use of flashback to structure the narrative from multiple perspectives, and the movie's examination of the Gulf War as a media war (CNN news footage punctuates the opening sequence and the military is shown cynically manipulating the public's sense of war), all indicate that the film is wider reaching in its aims.

The difficulty of representing the Gulf War, and perhaps war in general post-Vietnam, leads *Courage Under Fire* to prefer the more nuanced moves of the legal investigation narrative to the generic template of the combat movie. Combat is shown in the film – a tank battle and a helicopter crash

Women in combat: *Courage Under Fire* (1996)

and rescue – but the action is shown retrospectively in fragments, reconstructed from memory through a series of subjective, unreliable flashbacks (a similar tentative narrative structure can be found in *Rules of
Engagement* (2000)). The key theme is one of confusion with any sense of
the actual events on the ground proving very difficult to establish and the
decision to structure the film in this way unsettles the building blocks of
war mythology – honour, bravery, comradeship – and gives the film some
critical edge.

The early portions of the film's narrative, as well as the struggle to make
the war meaningful at a time when the war itself was far from resolved,
ensures that the film 'presents an image of the Gulf War as troubling and
ambiguous, with long-lasting consequences' (Sturken 1997: 137). Or, as
Susan E. Linville puts it, the film articulates 'the complex relationships
among trauma, truth, and the political/military manipulation of the media,
as well as of ethics, gender and combat' (2000: 106).

Inevitably, the film does work towards the resolution of this uncertainty
and the consolidation of a sense of war as progressive, just and, if waged for
the right reasons, ennobling. This shift from uncertainty about war to a recuperation of war's possibility can be seen in the film's negotiation of gender.
While the military is shown to be blind to race – Serling faces no prejudice
– the film finds most of its dramatic tension in Walden's experience as a

woman in the military. Her role as a soldier registers unsettlement as she struggles with the difficult decision to leave a daughter behind as she goes to war and also faces a mutinous crew hostile to being commanded by a woman. The film controls this uncertainty by adopting a fairly conventional ideological gendering overall. As Linville argues,

> Walden is unequivocally idealised as a single mother both in the descriptions that her parents provide and in the shots that juxtapose her with her daughter, Anne Marie. Even Walden's soldierly acts of violence are implicitly motivated by maternal protectiveness towards her crew, a domestication of female aggression that tends to render that aggression socially acceptable. (2000: 114)

Also, the film ultimately 'effaces the experience of Walden, allowing her no subjective point of view, telling her story only as a marker of an ensemble of troubled and traumatised male relationships' (2000: 107). Walden's story is sidelined, something mirrored in the representation of the Iraqis who are 'presented as anonymous bodies, mere props for war games and internecine conflicts' (Sturken 1997: 137). In fact, the structural relationship is such that Serling's trauma and subsequent recovery direct attention away from 'the particular political conditions and implications of Walden's demise and towards Serling's acts of remembrance, understanding, and contrition' (Linville 2000: 107). This is perhaps the film's most crucial move in which contemporary anxiety with regard to war is alleviated by being figured first in relation to gender (a problem, but a manageable one), but then, quickly, in relation to the therapeutic moves of the Vietnam War movie (as described in chapter three).

This ideological direction can be seen in the use of fire imagery in the film, and in particular the dropping of napalm to destroy a crashed American helicopter. The napalm marks a haunting event (the burning alive of Walden as she fights a rearguard action) that leads to experiences of psychological turmoil and guilt in those who witnessed it, shown in the film by mourning, drug addiction and suicide. As Linville suggests:

> napalm signals a double flashback, both to the trauma-laden scene of Walden's demise and to the US history in Vietnam and its legacy of loss and shattered manhood ... Indeed, the flames that kill Boylar

[in the 'friendly fire' incident] and haunt Serling in his dreams visually echo the film's napalm imagery and thereby reinforce the sweeping symbolic dimensions of Serling's quest. (2000: 109)

Although the spectre of Vietnam is in play, and indicates an uncertainty with regards to war in the contemporary period, Serling's quest is ultimately successful and the film's narrative is resolved via a final flashback that shows Walden behaving heroically under fire. In this flashback Hollywood's realism finally asserts authority over the hyperreality of the news coverage and the subjective, unreliable memories of the participants. Similarly, we also discover that Serling, although responsible for the 'friendly fire' incident, was responding pragmatically and professionally to an impossible situation in which Iraqi tanks had infiltrated American lines. This discovery enables Serling to resolve his own personal problems – writing a favourable report of Walden's actions, visiting Boylar's parents, and paying tribute to the war dead at Arlington National Cemetery – and in doing so recuperates any residual and qualified sense of the Vietnam conflict as well as allaying the implicit critiques of the contemporary US military put in play by the earlier narrative. In this way the film continues the process of rescripting the disruptive cultural memory of the Vietnam War as well as orchestrating a sympathetic mode of remembrance for the Gulf War. More crucially it paves the way for a renewal of a more positive sense of war's possibility in the contemporary period.

The greatest generation: Saving Private Ryan

No clearer evidence is needed of this new and more positive sense of war than the return of World War II to cinema screens in the late 1990s. *Saving Private Ryan* shows the D-Day landings and the American advance into France in 1944. The film tapped into a strongly celebratory view of World War II, raking in huge profits and quickly becoming the focal point for a large-scale process of commemoration. The movie opens with a shot of the Stars and Stripes. The weathered material and washed out cinematography suggest that the American flag post-Vietnam is still a relatively problematic signifier. However, what is crucial is that the flag is still flying. The traumatic disruptions of American history (*Amistad* (1997), another of Spielberg's history films, is one of the few Hollywood movies to acknowledge slavery)

Faded Stars and Stripes: *Saving Private Ryan* (1998)

have been sufficiently reconciled to allow a symbol of a unified American nationalism to guide the viewer into the film's action.

The flag is followed by a scene composed of stately, funereal tracking shots showing James Ryan (Matt Damon/James Young) walking through row upon row of white gravestones. Like the coda at the close of *Schindler's List* (1993) showing the surviving Schindler Jews at Oskar Schindler's grave in Jerusalem, and like the direct, imperative titles that introduce the World War II combat movie, this device activates discourse of sacrifice, mourning and national pride. The Vietnam War movies, *Hamburger Hill, Gardens of Stone* (1987) and *In Country* (1989) have opening sequences that are useful corollaries to this way of describing war. Michael Hammond argues that these scenes make the film's project explicit: 'it is a celluloid memorial' (2002: 69).

The 1994 anniversary of the D-Day landings, during which Bill Clinton walked the Normandy beaches in contemplation, had triggered a more general cultural fascination with World War II. In the political rhetoric of presidential speeches, the endlessly-looped television documentaries, and the nonfiction books dominating the bestseller lists, World War II has been constructed as a 'mythic, edenic moment when the entire nation bent itself to victory over evil and barbarism (Auster 2002: 104). The opening of *Saving Private Ryan* self-consciously interacts with this wider cultural memory and commemoration of World War II.

As Ryan draws towards a grave of particular significance we are shown that he is with his extended family, though they remain in the background of the shot. On reaching the grave Ryan breaks down, and as his family rush to offer support he asks, 'Have I been good?' It is a question that frames the movie, and as Ryan searches for an answer we hear the sound of battle. It is a familiar Spielberg sound match and in this case it cues a flashback to the moment just before the attack on Omaha Beach. Past and present here are shown to overlap, with history figured as a dynamic force which shapes the present, and to which we are beholden. The temporal and spatial shift is momentarily self-reflexive as Ryan makes direct eye contact with the viewer, and this intense moment of introspection marks the action of the film as a memory in the mind's eye of a World War II veteran, and encourages the audience to think of the war according to the thread of personal experience. The response of World War II veterans to the film, which has been largely favourable, has reinforced this framework in which survivor-testimony *authorises* a particular description of a historical event, helping to validate claims to historical accuracy as well as prompting a celebratory and self-consciously deferential reception for the film.

The key to the transition into battle is shock. Ryan's subjective point of view is immediately conflated with that of Capt. Miller (Tom Hanks) who we see first in a brief scene in a landing craft (Miller's hand shakes as he takes

War graves: *Saving Private Ryan* (1998)

a drink of water, a sign crucial to the later narrative that he is suffering post-traumatic stress). As the doors of the landing craft open two-thirds of the men on board are killed by machine-gun fire. What follows is a *tour de force* of immersive filmmaking showing graphic depictions of death and injury, a sense of the randomness of fatalities on a modern battlefield, the breakdown of command, and the impossibility of following the coded behaviours of bravery and self-sacrifice. All this along with something of the sense of battle: terrible, total and all encompassing.

A number of factors are important in generating this immersive sense of war. Like the flag that marks the opening sequence, the attack on the beach is shot in faded green earth tones and with the grainy definition of 1940s 16mm colour film. Cinematographer Janusz Kaminski emulated 1940s film stock by applying Technicolor's ENR process (a process that creates greater contrast, darker colours and desaturation) as well as removing modern lens coatings designed to reduce flare. The degree of shutter was also changed from 180 degrees to 45 degrees, which had the effect of making the film crisper and more staccato. These technical choices helped emulate the cinematography of World War II documentaries such as *The Battle of San Pietro* and *With the Marines at Tarawa* (1944).

In interview, Spielberg and Kaminski have also acknowledged the influence of Robert Capa's famous photographs of D-day. Capa's photographs, blurred because the negatives were accidently 'cooked' by picture editors in London, were presented to newspaper readers as indexical signs of the fear and chaos felt by those involved on the assault on the beach, their poor quality a sign of the severity of the fighting. By re-enacting these photographs and their attendant sense of chaos and catastrophe, the viewer is encouraged to understand the action as somehow indexically linked (that is, directly connected with) the events of 6 June 1944. This strategy (previously utilised to similar effect in *Platoon*, described in chapter three) makes particularly clear the way in which war cinema thrives on the mixing of fictional and nonfictional forms. It has the further effect of producing a powerful feeling of involvement in the audience and on the film's release many reviewers praised the first part of the film as a thoroughly 'authentic', 'accurate' and 'realistic' depiction of the landings at Omaha.

The film uses the full resources of contemporary cinema to maintain this sense of realism and immersion. The basic deep grammar of the classical Hollywood style – Miller as a key point of orientation, cross-cutting between German firing positions high on the bluff and US Army positions on the beach, and occasional deployment of an omniscient camera – does lend shape to the opening sequence. However, most of the other camera techniques work to disorient the viewer. The camera is mobile, often hand-held and subject to the concussions of nearby explosions. Mud, blood and gore hit the camera lens and obscure the viewer's vision, drawing attention to the film apparatus. From all directions and through sound and image, the experience of battle is a cacophony of danger pushing from all sides. The camera struggles through the killing zone and as we identify with this perspective (an imagined documentarist struggling to survive?) we find ourselves mired in the modern battlefield.

The staging of the action in this way is corroborated by the film's sound design that deploys a densely layered soundtrack that exploits the three-dimensionality of multiple-channel 'surround' sound. The action on screen is often preempted by the sound of 'incoming' shells or machine-gun fire and these sounds actively direct the viewer's attention to the next key move in the action as well as ensuring all off-screen space is perceived as deadly and dangerous. Robert Stam argues that in this completely immersive cinema, 'the spectator is "in" the image rather than confronted by it' (quoted in Maltby 2003: 259). The fleeting glimpses of eviscerations, mutilations and convulsions to which special effects coordinators Neil Corbould

The viewer as witness/survivor: *Saving Private Ryan* (1998)

and Gary Rydstronm submit the human body build into a picture of gruesome catastrophe, underwriting the sense of sacrifice and commitment displayed by the troops. It is significant that a large amount of the effects used were physical effects intended to emphasise the corporeality of the war scenario. Performance is governed by a similar logic. Dialogue is often drowned out by artillery fire and because the movie uses (at the time of the film's release) largely unknown actors, we do not know who is expendable in narrative terms and as a result the desire for identification is often brutally disrupted by random and bloody death.

By these means the film works hard to construct what might be labelled the 'endangered gaze'. The field of vision offered to the viewer ensures an intensely subjective point of view equivalent to the soldiers on the beach and the space off-screen, outside this field of vision, is full of threat from all directions through machine-gun fire, artillery, mines and enemy snipers (see Sobchack 1984: 297). Whereas most ways of understanding the pleasures inherent in Hollywood movies tend to focus on mastery (the description of Allied superiority and capability in *The Longest Day*, for example), the opening sequence of *Saving Private Ryan* thrives (at least for the first fifteen minutes or so) on terror and incomprehension.

Spielberg is quoted as saying: 'My hope in doing this is somehow to resensitise audiences to how bad it was for the men who survived, as well as for those who perished'. Hammond notes that the film 'addresses its audience as "survivors/consumers" plunged into the carnage of history' (2002: 69). Survivor testimony would seem to be the defining trope here with the film's opening sequence carefully designed to encourage the viewer to feel that they now have an intimate, lived sense of the event. (It is no coincidence that Spielberg presides over the Survivors of the Shoah Visual History Foundation, an organisation devoted to collating and archiving Holocaust-survivor testimony).

The consequences of describing war in this way are wide-reaching. First, it has a similar effect to the 'victory in defeat' paradigm found in World War II movies like *Wake Island* and *Bataan*, whereby the brutal violence directed towards American troops, as well as their bravery in facing this violence, justifies the wider military campaign and war in general. Second, this sense of trauma underwrites and authenticates the lived experience of the soldiers who experienced the battle. Their experience is presented as authoritative and precludes any critical questioning of the war. Third, trauma is a dominant cultural trope in contemporary American culture post-Vietnam. As shown in the analysis of Vietnam War movies in chapter three this trope ensures that historical events are thoroughly psychologised thereby eliding the contradictions, ambiguities and difficulties of history. As a result history is understood in very limited terms in relation to an individual traumatic experience that, with the imposition of the right thera-peutic narrative, can be overcome and resolved. Thus the description of the war as traumatic in this way synthesises very specific elements of the experience and memory of World War II into a robust strategy for thinking about war in general in the contemporary period. It is a strategy that, as this chapter will go on to detail, gains an even greater purchase on the contemporary cultural imagination of war in the aftermath of the terrorist attacks of 11 September 2001.

Once off the beach the movie is premised on a search for Ryan, a soldier whose three brothers have been killed during the D-day landings (the plot is loosely based on the true case of the Sullivan brothers, all five of whom were killed when the USS Juneau sank in the Pacific on 13 November 1942). The patrol assembled for the mission includes Miller (whose identity forms the basis for a betting syndicate amongst the men but who turns out to be a school teacher), a working-class Italian, a Brooklyn loner, a Nazi-hating Jew, an east-coast intellectual, a devout southern sharpshooter, a compas-sionate medic and a seasoned veteran. The members of the patrol are all shown to be brave and competent soldiers who, in various demonstrations of dutiful behaviour, perform conventional war movie heroics. The make-up of the patrol and the film's vignettes of heroic action mark how the film has broken free from revisionist accounts of World War II made in the wake of the Vietnam War (*The Dirty Dozen*, for example) and instead riffs on the combat movie of the 1940s and 1950s whose propagandist constructions of the war chime more readily with contemporary sensibilities. The men's protest at the incongruous nature of their mission is resolved by Miller who reminds them they are fighting to get home to their families (a common formulation in the contemporary war movie, writ particularly large in the Vietnam War movie *We Were Soldiers*) and by Ryan himself, who upon being found refuses to be evacuated.

The film does contain some hesitancy with regards to war and its effects. The most ambiguous character in the patrol is Cpl. Upham (Jeremy Davis) who has arrived in Normandy as a translator and as part of the second wave. Significantly, he has been spared the carnage of the beach and is not yet 'blooded'. Upham quotes Emerson's famous 1838 lecture 'War':

War educates the sense, calls into action the will. Perfects the physical constitution, brings men into such swift and close collision in critical moments, so man measures man.

It is a sentiment the film ultimately endorses but it is not yet something Upham fully understands. In a key early sequence Upham rails in defence of civilised values, protesting to Miller at the planned execution of a German prisoner nicknamed 'Steamboat Willie' (Joerg Stadler). However, later, in battle, Upham's lack of bravery leads to the death of Pvt. Mellish (Adam Goldberg) in a disturbing scene in which a German soldier eases a knife into his chest while begging him not to struggle. Characterisation here is used to show something of the complex, contradictory motivations and feelings of an individual thrown into combat.

This strand of the narrative has further significance. Earlier in the film Mellish has proudly claimed himself Jewish to a column of German POWs, thereby activating a powerful discourse relating to the Nazi Holocaust. The belief that World War II was fought to prevent Nazi human rights abuses is now commonplace and as a result the Holocaust has become the primary cipher through which the wider war is understood (Piehler 1995: 148). This interpretation of the war feeds into the scene of Mellish's death, giving Upham's culpability greater resonance. As such the logic of the film implies that principle is all very well but that principle must always be backed by emphatic action. The film resolves the scenario by showing Upham in a later scene reneging on his earlier stated principles and choosing to kill 'Steamboat Willie' in order to assert his authority over a party of surrendering German soldiers. This whole narrative thread reads as a qualified articulation of how morality and progressive principle will necessarily require a willingness to kill. Put simply, civilisation is shown to require war. As such, *Saving Private Ryan* chimes with the late 1990s tendency to make humanitarianism central to any rationale for war.

This creed is embodied in the character of Miller. Like Upham, Miller displays the characteristics of erudition, principle and morality; yet in Miller the value system is tempered by war and steeled with resolve. Miller is aware of the cost involved in holding principles and displays the necessary pragmatism and self-discipline to see the mission through. In a desparate last stand to hold back a German counter-attack Miller faces down a German tank armed only with a pistol. Tom Hanks' star persona – with its measured balance of physical awkwardness, reticence, good-natured intelligence, ordinariness, and so on – meshes perfectly with the character of Miller and this sequence demonstrates precisely how the psychologically unstable characters of *Apocalypse Now* and the superhero of the *Rambo* films have now been replaced by the image of an ordinary man behaving in an extraordinary way. In this sequence Miller (suffering the trauma of previous heroic actions and at the film's close sacrificing his life to the cause) becomes paradigmatic of America's self-image in the contemporary period: a benevolent, caring, altruistic force waging war only reluctantly and for humanitarian reasons. As he dies Miller asks that Ryan 'earn' the sacrifice that has been made by the men, repeating the dominant formulation that a generation sacrificed their lives for the freedom of future generations.

Ending where it began, the film returns to the war grave of Capt. Miller. Ryan asks his wife if he has been a 'good man'. The question remains unanswered but Ryan's extended family surround him, and without words, reassure him that he has indeed lived up to the responsibility passed to him by the sacrifice of these men. The film requires that the viewer pose Ryan's question as a civic and collective one. 'Have I led a good life?' becomes

'Tell me I'm a good man': *Saving Private Ryan* (1998)

'Have we led a good life?' Ultimately the film suggests Ryan, and America, has carried this burden successfully, and this reassurance surely lifts some further weight off the continued guilt felt with regards to the Vietnam War, as well as ameliorating the facts of America's reluctant commitment to, and limited success in, 'humanitarian' foreign policy engagements in Somalia, Bosnia and Kosovo in the 1990s.

The HBO television series *Band of Brothers* (2001), executive produced by Steven Spielberg and Tom Hanks, forms an aesthetically- and thematically-linked intertext to *Saving Private Ryan*. A brief consideration of *Band of Brothers* throws further light on the powerful mechanisms for imagining war established by *Saving Private Ryan*. The series takes its starting point as D-day and follows a company of American soldiers through the latter stages of the war from tough fighting in the Ardennes, through the liberation of the western European concentration camps (Bergen-Belsen in particular) to the taking of Hitler's Eagle's Nest at Berteschgarden. It is a symbolic narrative of bravery, sacrifice, momentum and purpose. The requisite trauma is supplied when the advance into Europe becomes bogged down at Bastogne.

Correspondences with *Saving Private Ryan* are clear enough. Each episode of *Band of Brothers* begins with documentary film of veteran's remembering their experiences of World War II, this time with none of the 'equivocal' relationship to their actions as that felt by many Vietnam veterans. Working in a similar register to the bookends of *Saving Private Ryan*, these testimonies give the fiction decisive authority and grant the ordinary soldier a kind of gatekeeper role governing 'access' to the wider event. The series is also filmed in the exact style of *Saving Private Ryan*, especially in its emulation of key newsreel and documentary films, in particular the harrowing episode showing the liberation of the Nazi death camps. Miller's role is echoed in the character of Maj. Winters (Damian Lewis), a Quaker and intellectual who reluctantly finds himself to be a successful warrior and leader. In their gentle religiosity, their reluctance to fight, but also in their complete mastery of the process of soldiering, Miller and Winters represent a particular liberal endorsement of war's progressive possibilities.

Band of Brothers is based on Stephen Ambrose's best-selling book of the same name. Ambrose's nonfiction is hugely popular and its success is in part due to its unapologetically heroic account of America's role in World War II. In *Citizen Soldiers*, Ambrose writes:

At the core, the American citizen soldiers knew the difference between right and wrong, and they didn't want to live in a world in which wrong prevailed. So they fought, and won, and we all of us, living and yet to be born, must be forever and profoundly grateful. (1997: 473)

Ambrose explicitly valorises the ordinary American who in their implicit goodness offers salvation to a world fallen victim to the ideologies of fascism and militarism. Ambrose describes how during World War II the sight of a squad of Soviet, German or Japanese soldiers brought terror to people's hearts because they 'meant rape, pillage, looting, wanton destruction, senseless killing' (1997: 486). He claims an exception:

a squad of GIs, a sight that brought the biggest smiles you ever saw to people's lips, and joy to their hearts. Around the world this was true, even in Germany, even – after September 1945 – in Japan. This was because GIs meant candy, cigarettes, C-rations, and freedom. America had sent the best of her young men around the world, not to conquer but to liberate, not to terrorise but to help. This was the great moment in our history. (Ibid.)

Ambrose's construction (clearly articulated in *Saving Private Ryan* and *Band of Brothers*) makes American exceptionalism explicit. Any evidence of the refusal of American conscripts to fight, mass desertions in the US Army in the European theatre, criminal behaviour in the ranks and American involvement in the black market of food, medical supplies and weapons, is studiously ignored (see Roeder 1993; Fussell 2004). Also effaced is the archly political management of the war by the American government – protecting American interests, balancing lobby groups and voter constituencies, brokering deals with allies, and so on. In its place we see what might be called the 'greatest generation' interpretation of World War II in which the war is seen in relation to the individual experience of dignified, honorable men, and through a nostalgic lens (Brokaw 2002). It is not necessary to enter into an argument over whether or not this version of World War II is misleading in historical terms (Paul Fussell labels it 'military-romanticism' (2004: xv)). It is enough simply to note that a 'Good War' fought for moral reasons and in which America was victorious has now replaced the Vietnam War as the paradigm within which war in general is now understood. As a result films like *Saving Private Ryan* and *Band of Brothers* (not to mention a whole host of tied-in computer games with titles such as *Medal of Honour*, *Combat Elite* and *Battleground Europe*), with their primary focus on the moral certainty of a particular version of World War II now conceal the edgy and complex war cinema of the late 1970s and early 1980s, pushing to the margins movies like *Apocalypse Now* and *Platoon,* which for all their shortcomings did show American culpability in racism, rape, murder and military incompetence. The war cinema of the late 1990s – for all its liberal hesitancy – subsumes these more complex and difficult visions of war, laying a foundation of sorts for real war in the contemporary period.

Remembrance and revenge: Pearl Harbor

The use of this nostalgic version of World War II to shape the contemporary cultural imagination of war can also be seen in the big-budget movie, *Pearl Harbor*. The attack on Pearl Harbor by Japanese naval forces on 7 December 1941 has left a considerable imprint on the war movie genre in films such as *December 7th*, *So Proudly We Hail*, *From Here To Eternity, Midway* and *Tora! Tora! Tora!* (1970). Marcia Landy notes how these varied films rely on similar narrative tropes:

> a dramatisation of the violation of innocence, a portrait of US victim-hood and of Japanese perfidy. The texts are constructed in elegiac fashion as a lament for the victims. While the survivors' accounts are replete with their detailed descriptions of horror accompanied by repeated images and reconstructions of the catastrophe, they are balanced by descriptions of extraordinary acts of heroism. (2004: 87)

Pearl Harbor, released to coincide with 60th anniversary commemorations of the attack and accompanied by two high-profile documentaries screened by the History Channel and National Geographic respectively, is no exception to the general formula. The film is predominantly a romance in which two childhood friends – Rafe McCawley (Ben Affleck) and Danny Walker (Josh Hartnett) – become combat pilots and compete for the love of a woman. The early scenes conform to a nostalgic vision of America in which the 1930s are signified by battered Levis jeans and old-style Coke bottles, all shot in glossy soft focus. Childhood is here used as a metaphor for an American state of innocence soon to be brutally shattered by the Japanese attack. Though more painterly in style *Saving Private Ryan* deploys something similar in its 'home front' sequences; the shot of the Ryans' mother receiving news of the death of her sons (based on Andrew Wyeth's painting 'Christina's World') nostalgically depicts an American rural idyll. The nostalgic tone of both films indicates a loss and longing for an earlier and simpler time in which Americans rallied to a single cause. It is no accident that this nostalgia for consensus coincides with a loss of political direction, marked in the 2000 election by a hung decision between Republican candidate George W. Bush Jr and Democrat Al Gore (a senate ruling would eventually give the election to Bush).

This nostalgia for the certainties of World War II extends to characterisation and *Pearl Harbor* is slavishly committed to gender constructions that emulate those found in 1940s war movies. The women in *Pearl Harbor* are shot with high gloss and glamour (Betty Grable and 1940s pin-ups are obvious points of reference) and characterised through their work as nurses, their willing subservience to men, and in their lack of any notable ambition. The construction of gender in this way confirms a conservative outlook, one that revels nostalgically in past certainties (even where these certainties, as shown in chapter two, have more to do with propagandist descriptions of women's experience rather than any reality).

Conventional gender stereotyping: *Pearl Harbor* (2001)

Identity in relation to race is treated in an equally conventional manner. In contrast to *Saving Private Ryan*, *Pearl Harbor* returns to the politically-correct balance found in 1940s war movies. The film shows Dory Miller (Cuba Gooding Jr), a black chef (one of the few positions open to black Americans in the US Navy in the 1940s), fighting valiantly during the Japanese attack. The narrative is awkward in its accommodation of Miller whose story remains tangential, but the ideological move is clear enough: the 'greatest generation' includes black Americans. In fact, their patriotism, altruism and ability to distinguish between good and evil, and the fact that *despite* their marginal position in American society they are still willing to defend their limited freedom to the death, make them the paradigm of the specific identity constructed by the 'greatest generation'-view of the war. *Tuskegee Airmen* (1995), a movie that tells the story of the first black fighter pilot squadron, displays this tendency writ large.

Any evidence of racial hatred in relation to the Japanese enemy is also played down. The Japanese are described even-handedly, their dedication and discipline acknowledged, and in contrast to the World War II combat movie the language used by the American characters to describe them is careful in its avoidance of racial slurs and diminutions. These strategies of representation, indicating a multi-racial togetherness in the American ranks and a lack of structural racism towards the Japanese, maintain a nostalgic vision by eliding any coherent sense of the actual historical situation, where, as chapter two demonstrated, racism was a structurally significant part of American society and the war effort. Both strategies are good examples of the appropriation of political correctness in the service of historical revision.

After a 90-minute set-up the romance narrative is placed on hold for a CGI-heavy reconstruction of the Japanese attack. These sequences constitute the core of the movie and in their commitment to an immersive experience of war they function in ways similar to the opening sequence of *Saving Private Ryan*. A key scene follows the fall line of a bomb as it zeroes in on an American warship. A computer-generated point-of-view shot places the viewer in the bomb's sights moments before detonation. The effect of this on the audience is, once again, to generate a profound sense of helplessness and a masochistic sense of identification with those caught up in war's violence as victims. Considering the use of strategic bombing as the primary weapon in American foreign policy interventions from the end of the Second World War to the present day (with the use of nuclear weapons on Hiroshima and Nagasaki unprecedented in the history of war), it is telling that the war cinema reverses these roles and places the American cinema-goer on the receiving end of a devastating bombing raid.

During the attack the various characters commit to the work of war unfailingly and heroically. In a hospital inundated with the wounded, heroic nurses work to heal while volunteers give blood. The film's moment of greatest pathos involves the death of a nurse (recalling at some level the narrative tropes of the World War I propaganda film) and the construction of outrage, togetherness, heroism and self-sacrifice reaches its apogee in a scene where Coca-Cola bottles are used for improvised blood transfusions.

The effect of this sequence – a spectacular of anti-American violence – shackles a sense of America as an undeserving victim to a renewal of the signifier war. Elisions around gender, race and the motives of the enemy have the effect of separating the traumatic nature of the attack from its historical context, turning it into a synthetic trauma available to be phrased and rephrased in relation to contemporary anxieties. Like the trauma of the opening sequences of *Saving Private Ryan*, the attack in *Pearl Harbor* generates a sense of America as under threat, imperiled by the unsafe space surrounding it but without presenting any historical particularity to this sense of threat.

The sequences showing the immediate aftermath of the attack linger on the destruction of the US naval fleet, with elegiac shots reminiscent of

Blood, gore and nostalgia: *Pearl Harbor* (2001)

funeral rituals offering time for introspection. These sequences – focusing in particular on the USS Arizona (in which 1,102 sailors were drowned and entombed, and which became a national monument in 1962) – tie the action to American's subsequent sense of the significance of events at Pearl Harbor. Like *Saving Private Ryan* the film offers itself to a process of mourning, commemoration and myth and this, combined with the activation of a synthetic trauma, explains how the film resonated so powerfully with the subsequent experience of the terrorist attacks of 11 September 2001.

Landy describes how in the aftermath of the terrorist attacks the central components of the Pearl Harbor narrative, including the reiteration of innocence violated, the language of trauma and the desire for retaliation against a faceless enemy (all deployed in *Pearl Harbor*, the movie) were called upon in newspaper and television coverage of 11 September (2004: 86–7). CBS News anchorman Dan Rather even went so far as to refer to the terrorist attacks on the World Trade Center and the Pentagon as 'the Pearl Harbor of terrorism' (quoted in Landy 2004: 79). A mythologised view of a key battle in World War II, cloaked in the moves of the contemporary war cinema, was used to understand a present-day emergency.

Saving Private Ryan and *Pearl Harbor*, in different ways, indicate how by the late 1990s the cultural imagination of war successfully reclaimed the idea of war as progressive, necessary and ennobling. It might be useful to think of *Saving Private Ryan* as a liberal argument for war, qualified as it is with themes of mourning, regret, trauma and psychological breakdown. On the other hand, *Pearl Harbor* in its more avowedly nostalgic approach and muscular celebration of combat deploys strategies for representing war most commonly articulated by the political right. Figured either way, recent wars have been understood according to a nostalgic and simplified view of America's experience in World War II rather than in relation to the conflict in Vietnam, a conflict with which they invariably have a great deal more in common.

Humanitarian war: Black Hawk Down

This reimagination of war from liberal and right-wing positions in the 1990s sees war as necessary and often progressive and this remains relatively unproblematic when it goes with the grain of cultural memory of World War II (a war now firmly lodged in the cultural imagination as a good war). The events on Omaha Beach and at Pearl Harbor, and the nostalgic longing for the very real threat of German fascism and Japanese militarism, offer a version of 'clear and present danger'. The films offer galvanising events through which consensus might be renewed and democratic politics redeemed. In this respect the war cinema of the late 1990s chimes with another significant cycle, the disaster movie, with films like *Independence Day* (1996), *Deep Impact* (1998) and *Armageddon* (1998) all registering a similar cultural tendency, the nostalgic longing for a powerful enemy or a threatening event (see Keane 2006). However, the contemporary period provided America with no such clear-cut adversaries. World War II and the Cold War were conflicts in which powerful competing ideological systems threatened America's sphere of influence. In contrast the complex wars fought in the post-Cold War period, often involving complex negotiations with international allies, could not be presented in such clear-cut binary terms. This new kind of war would prove a difficult sell for Hollywood.

Behind Enemy Lines (2001), a loose remake of the Vietnam War movie *BAT-21* (1988), uses a careful construction of space to simplify and reverse the power relations bearing on the conflict in the former Yugoslavia. American pilot, Lt. Chris Burnett (Owen Wilson) is shot down after taking photographic evidence of war crimes. Once on the ground Burnett is hunted by the Serbian military. Disadvantaged by geography and left stranded due to the complex political machinations of NATO and the UN, he is forced to rely on his own initiative and resolve in order to avoid capture. Like the role reversal marked by the attack sequences in *Pearl Harbor*, the dominance of US air power is neatly turned around, and viewers are instead asked to adopt a position of powerlessness and immersion in a dangerous combat scenario.

While escaping from the Serb military Burnett stumbles into a mass war grave, only evading capture by covering himself in dead bodies and mud. In another key sequence Burnett enters the enclave of Hac where he (almost) suffers the same fate as the Bosnian Muslims there who are being exterminated by Serb forces. In these sequences Burnett, and America, appropriate the experience of the victims of ethnic cleansing and motivated by this experience the film shows the American military finding the will to fight driven primarily by the impulse to revenge. As Burnett is lifted to safety with photographic evidence of war crimes, helicopter gunships decimate Serb positions. The film's ending reframes military intervention

Unearthing war crimes: *Behind Enemy Lines* (2001)

as clear cut humanitarianism and rationalises the use of massive retributive force as justified revenge.

Very similar strategies inform *Black Hawk Down*, which shows American
soldiers intervening in civil conflict in Somalia. According to the film's
opening credits the US-led UN intervention is a humanitarian one to bring
to an end to a decade-long famine. A mission to arrest key rebel leaders
goes wrong and Army Special Rangers become stranded in hostile parts of
Mogadishu. As a rescue operation is mounted two Black Hawk helicopters
are shot down and two convoys meander lost and under attack through
the Byzantine streets. Like the Bosnian countryside in *Behind Enemy Lines*,
Mogadishu is constructed as chaotic and threatening, beyond the reach
of commanders, intelligence reports and tactical strategising. The unsafe
space of the city is a space in which atrocities happen and a space that
America must take control of and civilise.

The film's figuring of the military engagement in this way – especially
through the character of Sgt. Matt Eversmann (Josh Hartnett) who manages
to keep his moral bearings in a chaotic combat situation – requires many
of the aspects clearly delimited in Mark Bowden's journalistic account of
the battle, upon which the film is based, to be left out. For instance, the
film does not show the indiscriminate killing of Somali civilians or the
taking of civilian hostages by American troops. The film also obscures the
massively disproportionate casualties that resulted from the indiscriminate
use of American military firepower. By once again reversing roles the film

searches for a way of describing a contemporary foreign policy engagement according to the moral certainties of the 1990s World War II combat movie in which brave and moral American soldiers respond to a severe and overwhelming threat from a perfidious and immoral enemy.

The end result of constructing space in this way is to dehumanise the people who inhabit that space (the Somalis are shown only as passive helpless victims or corrupt bloodthirsty fanatics) and also to endorse strategies of long-range warfare, especially aerial bombardment, that annihilates this unsafe space, making it safe for American liberal democracy while also protecting the differentially-valued lives of American soldiers.

All this justification and endorsement of war and war's progressive role even permits a return of Vietnam to the cinema screens in the contemporary period. *We Were Soldiers* is a nostalgic endorsement of American involvement in Southeast Asia that would have been unimaginable a decade earlier. The film – based on a successful memoir – focuses on the character of Col. Hal Moore (Mel Gibson) who fights a clever tactical battle against overwhelming North Vietnamese Army (NVA) forces. The film displays no concession to the dominant orthodoxy of the war cinema of the 1970s and 1980s that showed the Vietnam War as an unsuccessful and morally questionable undertaking. Instead American military strategy is shown to be credible, heroic and morally right.

Moore's confident warrior father-figure contrasts sharply with, say, Willard's alienation in *Apocalypse Now*, or the lonely struggles of John

The third world as unsafe space: *Black Hawk Down* (2001)

Rambo in the *Rambo* films. The film's opening shot shows Moore's epic family driving in the car together in sing-song; another cut away contrasts Moore's combat boots with his daughter's tiny feet as they pray together. Asked by his youngest daughter: 'What is war?' Moore replies, drawing on Gibson's awkward, humble comic persona: 'Something that shouldn't happen, but it does, and ... erm ... it's when some people in another country, or any country, try to take the lives of people, and then soldiers like your daddy have to, you know, it's my job to go over there and stop 'em.' Similarly, in Moore's address of his troops on the eve of deployment to Vietnam he describes the Army according to a philosophy of inclusiveness and integration and claims that the Army is 'what family was always meant to be'. By these means the family is somehow shown to motivate America's war in Vietnam in the contemporary war cinema's most simplistic articulation of war and war's purpose.

In a familiar enough move by now the imperative to wage war is governed by a righteous anger stemming from the movie's gratuitous portrayal of American soldiers machine-gunned by NVA regulars in endless, predictable slow-motion. Surrounded by enemy troops America is once again shown to be the victim, with its forces outnumbered by a more powerful enemy. The Alamo is referred to, tapping into the powerful trope of victory in defeat (the Alamo is also evoked in *Saving Private Ryan* and *Black Hawk Down*). Motivated by this violent affront, Moore tricks the enemy into the open through audacious tactics and then calls in an air strike in which NVA troops are killed *en masse*. It is a telling image, a fantasy of airborne omnipotence and technologically-empowered retribution. Ultimately, the film's celebration of Moore's unbridled masculinity and tactical cleverness imply that with more men like Moore, America's fate in Vietnam would have been significantly different.

It is telling that Hollywood's most recent big-budget Vietnam War movie, in its elegiac embrace of military ritual, its obfuscation of the reasons for American involvement, its use of gender stereotypes and the trope of victory in defeat, phrases war according to the positive formulations of the most jingoistic genre mainstays. The title of the movie – *We Were Soldiers* – captures a nostalgic sense of wholeness in the past, when soldiering was a honourable activity and it is this general sense of war that persists as the primary point of orientation with regards war in the contemporary period.

The contemporary cultural imagination of war

To draw this chapter, and the book, to a close I wish to identify the key component parts of the contemporary cultural imagination of war. These component parts fall under the following headings: point of view, identity, morality and memory. I hope that a brief description of each of these will provide the reader with a series of staging posts from which to embark on further inquiry into the war movie genre and its political effects.

Point of view – Pierre Sorlin describes how war movies show war 'as the sum of heroic actions carried out by a handful of individuals' (1994: 360). This focus on individual experience is not in itself a hindrance to a complex understanding of war. For example, during the Vietnam War those protesting the war often focused on the 'ambivalent location of the GI as simultaneously the agent and victim of imperialist politics' (James 1985: 42). In *The Thin Red Line* (1998), one of the few intelligent and ambitious war movies made in the contemporary period, different points of view – Pvt. Witt's (James Caviezel) existential dreamer, Sgt. Edward Welsh's (Sean Penn) cynical individualist and Lt. Col. Gordon Tall's (Nick Nolte) desperate middle manager – interact to build a complex and critical sense of war (Hammond 2002: 70–2; see also Patterson 2003). In general, though, the war cinema's focus on individual experience is profoundly reductive, acting as a premise for partial sightedness and lack of historical framing.

In *A Walk in the Sun*, Pvt. McWilliams (Serling Holloway) gripes that 'the only trouble [with war] is you can't see nothing'. Later in the film McWilliams climbs up over a ridge carrying a pair of binoculars in an attempt to get a sense of the bigger picture. He is immediately shot dead by an enemy sniper, leading Basinger to note that 'he sees war, and thus becomes its victim' (1986: 148). McWilliams' fate is indicative of how, if the complex and political motivations behind war are to be elided, the cinemagoer must be discouraged from seeing, and hence thinking, too much. *Black Hawk Down* is only the most recent example of how a deeply political myopia restricts audience access to any of the wider senses of America's strategic involvement in Somalia, or of the complex and compromised nature of war as humanitarian peacekeeping in the contemporary period.

In Errol Morris' erudite documentary *The Fog of War* (2004), a beautifully crafted animated insert shows statistics rather than bombs being dropped from B-52s over the Vietnamese countryside. This eloquent image is used to illustrate Robert McNamara's (a key architect of US foreign policy during the Vietnam War) reflections on the ways in which statistical analysis of military strategy determined the way war was waged. Counter-pointing this image with McNamara's honest reflections on war indicates how any productive cultural imagination of war will require this mixed sense of things, a constant matching of the limited human experience of war to those structures – economy, technology, national interest and so on – that give war is wider shape and determine its outcome. It is an image with no corollary in the contemporary war cinema.

The most recent cycle of war movies – especially *Saving Private Ryan* and *Pearl Harbor* – has ensured that the experience and memory of veterans who fought in World War II has become the primary portal through which access is gained to that global, and profoundly complex, historical event. *Jarhead* focalises the first Gulf War through the limited horizon of Anthony Snoffard (Jake Gyllenhall), a scout sniper who never actually fires his weapon. Once consigned to the realm of personal experience in this way, war is bound by an economy that shows conflict as a total, overwhelming psychological experience. Phrased in this way history is understood through the limited personal narratives of spiritual growth and therapeutic transcendence that are so ubiquitous in American culture. The comparison made between 9/11 and the attack on Pearl Harbor is a good example of how a mythologised version of World War II, bounded by the limited horizons of survivor testimony, has shaped our understanding of contemporary events. *Flags of Our Fathers* (2006), produced by Steven Spielberg and directed by Clint Eastwood, and based on James Bradley's non-fiction bestseller, tells the stories of the soldiers involved in the flag-raising on Iwo Jima, and indicates that the limited experience of the war veteran will continued to anchor the contemporary cultural imagination of war.

Identity – Locating war primarily in relation to individual experience in this way has further effects, which bring us to the second key component of the contemporary cultural imagination of war: identity. This is seen most clearly in the war movie's dependence on a prejudicial construction of cultural otherness, in which an American identity is forged in relation to the threat of an enemy who is alien and dangerous. John Dower has described how the representation of the Japanese in World War II combat movies evidences a long history of racist figuring of cultural difference. He notes how the Japanese were

> saddled with racial stereotypes that Europeans had applied to non-whites for centuries: during the conquest of the New World, the slave trade, the Indian Wars in the US, the colonisation of Asia and Africa, and so on. (1986: 10)

In propaganda movies made during World War II American values and rationales for war were defined over and against this version of cultural otherness. These strategies also persisted into the later war movie genre. As Dower notes,

> these patterns of thinking were transferred laterally and attached to the new enemies of the Cold War era: the Soviets and Chinese communists, the Korean foe of the early 1950s, the Vietnamese enemy of the 1960s and 1970s. (Ibid.)

This prejudicial view, although tempered somewhat by political correctness and historical revision, still informs the war cinema of the contemporary period. War continues to be shown – in films such as *Pearl Harbor, Saving Private Ryan, Behind Enemy Lines* and *Black Hawk Down* – as an existential battle between humane, moral individuals and a faceless, fanatical, inhumane enemy.

Even a liberal movie such as *Courage Under Fire*, so sensitive to the nuance of identity and ethnicity when describing the tensions within the American military, resorts to strategies in which the Iraqis are shown as faceless, cruel and ineffectual. Some subtlety can be found in *Three Kings* (1999), the most satirical war movie of the late 1990s, in which Iraqis are differentiated – shown as Saddam loyalists, Kurdish rebels and reluctant conscripts – but even in this complex film the *dénouement* describes the Gulf War in simplistic patronising terms (Hammond 2002: 72–3).

The corrolary of a prejudicial construction of racial difference is a powerful nationalistic discourse running the hundred years from *Tearing Down the Spanish Flag* to the flag that flies in the opening sequence of *Saving Private Ryan*. The war cinema presents America as the world's 'indispensible nation' unparalleled in its commitment to freedom and democracy. Internationalist descriptions of America's role in World War II common to the genre in the 1940s and 1950s have given way to a thoroughly Americanised version of the war (as the controversy regarding the film *U-571* (2000) demonstrates). America's nationalistic claim to these important ideals is not completely unfounded. Yet these principles sit uncomfortably with America's wars including genocidal military campaigns against its indigenous people, imperialism in Latin America, and the covert support of barbaric regimes in many parts of the world, all conducted in order to protect economic and strategic interests and all requiring considerable flexibility in America's stated principles of freedom and democracy. A national identity that is to be of value will not repress this history in order to produce a mythologised version of America and Americanness. This is precisely what this book has shown the contemporary war cinema to do.

One of the further limitations of the point of view offered by the war cinema is its privileging of male experience. From *Bataan* to *We Were Soldiers*, propagandist and patriotic versions of the warrior myth rely on a construction of a form of masculinity in which men behave with discipline, capability and bravery according to strict codes of duty, honour and heroism. Where women, and the 'feminine', appear in the war movie it is almost without fail in a subordinate role, most often to insure the masculine ideal. Once again, *Bataan* and *We Were Soldiers* show the process in stark

War as male experience: *Courage Under Fire* (1996)

relief, though it can be found in more nuanced representations of gender and the military such as *Courage Under Fire*.

It is true that this masculine ideal was destabilised by the experience of Vietnam. However, as this book has demonstrated much ideological work has subsequently been done to restore the ideal and give it renewed prominence in relation to war and to social experience more generally. According to Susan Jeffords, patriarchy underwrites war and war underwrites patriarchy and the contemporary war cinema ensures that both are ultimately endorsed as essential, binding and positive elements of our social reality (see 1989: xi–xv and 180–2).

Morality – Perhaps the most significant component part of the contemporary cultural imagination of war is its avowedly moral viewpoint. The moral universe constructed by almost all war movies, in which the battle, or campaign, or wider war is posed as a struggle between elemental forces of good and evil (with World War II and the Nazi Holocaust the most obvious case) severely limits the cultural imagination of war. According to this way of thinking Americans fight for survival and virtue, and only when gravely wronged. Of course, this moral universe is called into question in the late 1970s by the experience of the Vietnam War, and reflected in the Vietnam War movie cycles of the late 1970s and 1980s. Yet even in films like *Apocalypse Now* the desire for a clear moral dimension to war persists as a sub-structure, a structure towards which the characters blindly stumble and strive. The successful revision of the experience of the Vietnam War allows a view of war as a crucible of moral action to be reclaimed in the post-Cold War period and all recent foreign policy commitments have been phrased in these moral (that is, humanitarian) terms. The problem with seeing and thinking about war in this way is that it blocks properly historical understanding of American strategy or political purpose, an understanding that can only come from an appreciation of the complex, self-interested, often economic, motivations influencing America's entry into wars past and present.

Memory – War is a key building block in the formation of cultural memory and the war movie genre is one of the primary ways in which past wars are recalled, re-enacted and rescripted. As the opening and closing sequences of *Saving Private Ryan* show, the war movie often self-consciously presents itself as a kind of celluloid memorial. In the contemporary period World War II has replaced the Vietnam War as the war that shapes contemporary thinking. For example, after the 11 September 2001 terrorist attack the famous photograph of US marines raising a flag on Iwo Jima, an image re-enacted in the World War II movie *Sands of Iwo Jima*, was restaged at Ground Zero. America's most enduring propaganda image of World War II, an image of moral rectitude, courageous military action and masculine capability that had worked to build a wartime consensus, resurfaced at the start of the twenty-first century in order to give shape to the experience of terrorist atrocity. In the years since 9/11 America's nostalgia for a 'greatest generation' who, according to films like *Saving Private Ryan* and *Band of Brothers*, fought the good fight and paved the way for democracy and freedom has been used to shape an ineffective humanitarian foreign policy (under Bill Clinton) and then to help justify and endorse the waging of wars in Afghanistan and Iraq (under George W. Bush). It seems that America's misapprehension of the complexity of these war scenarios is in part due to a reliance on the 'military-romanticism' that govern contemporary understanding of World War II. The cultural imagination of war in the contemporary period relies on a kind of faulty memory, the unreliability of which the war cinema has undoubtedly contributed.

***

The film industry has a long history of producing movies that seek to justify and endorse war (often with guidance from governmental propaganda agencies and support from the military) and in describing war in this way these movies shape and consolidate the general sense that war is a valid and productive political and economic tool. The number of films functioning as genuine critique – *All Quiet on the Western Front, Paths of Glory,* possibly *Apocalypse Now* – are few and far between and in general the war cinema forms the ground upon which the benefits and justifications for war are argued out and shown to be convincing.

As a result the cultural imagination of war is predisposed to conceive war as a positive and necessary part of human experience. This belief that war is just and necessary is itself a prerequisite to the waging of war. Hence, the cultural imagination of war by Hollywood, whilst in many respects a wholly cultural activity, is also constitutive of war in very real terms. As such, a spectrum of experience links our trip to the cinema to see the latest war movie with war-torn Baghdad or Kabul.

I hope this book has shown that it is important to be suspicious of Hollywood's cultural imagination of war in which a myopic view of the past – predicated on a limited point of view, a prejudicial and nationalistic construction of cultural and ideological otherness, a reconstructed masculine capability, and a profound nostalgia for a mythologised version of World War II – has become justification for war in the present.

FILMOGRAPHY

The films listed below constitute a list of all titles discussed in this book, as well as many of the most important films within the genre of war cinema. For a fuller filmography see Curley & Wetta 1992.

Above and Beyond (Melvin Frank and Norman Panama, 1952, US)
Action in the North Atlantic (Lloyd Bacon, 1943, US)
Air Force (Howard Hawks, 1943, US)
All Quiet on the Western Front (Lewis Milestone, 1930, US)
All Quiet on the Western Front (Delbert Mann, 1979, US)
Americanization of Emily, The (Arthur Hiller, 1964, US)
Amistad (Steven Spielberg, 1997, US)
Anderson Platoon, The (Pierre Schoendorffer, 1966, France)
Antwone Fisher (Denzel Washington, 2002, US)
Apocalypse Now (Francis Ford Coppola, 1979, US)
Armageddon (Michael Bay, 1998, US)
Attack! (Robert Aldrich, 1956, US)
Attack on a Chinese Mission Station, Bluejackets to the Rescue (James
    Williamson, 1901, US)
Back to Bataan (Edward Dmytryk, 1945, US)
Bamboo Prison, The (Lewis Seiler, 1955, US)
BAT-21 (Peter Markle, 1988, US)
Bataan (Tay Garnett, 1943, US)
Battle Circus (Richard Brooks, 1953, US)
Battle Cry (Raoul Walsh, 1955, US)
Battle Cry of Peace, The (J. Stuart Blackton and Wilfrid North, 1915, US)
Battleground (William A. Wellman, 1949, US)
Battle Hymn (Douglas Sirk, 1957, US)

Battle of Cupidovitch, The (John Francis Dillon, 1916, US)
Battle of Gettysbury (Thomas Ince, 1914, US)
Battle of Midway, The (John Ford, 1942, US)
Battle of Nations, The (Allen Curtis, 1915, US)
Battle of San Pietro, The (John Huston, 1945, US)
Battle of Shiloh, The (Joseph W. Smiley, 1914, US)
Battle of the Bulge (Ken Annakin, 1965, US)
Battle of the Yalu (American Mutoscope and Biograph Co., 1904, US)
Be Neutral (Francis Ford, 1914, US)
Beach Red (Cornell Wilde, 1967, US)
Behind Enemy Lines (John Moore, 2001, US)
Behind the Door (Irwin Willat, 1919, US)
Best Years of Our Lives, The (William Wyler, 1946, US)
Big Lift, The (George Seaton, 1951, US)
Big Parade, The (King Vidor, 1925, US)
Big Red One, The (Samuel Fuller, 1980, US)
Birdy (Alan Parker, 1984, US)
Birth of a Nation, The (D. W. Griffith, 1915, US)
Black Hawk Down (Ridley Scott, 2001, US)
Black Sunday (John Frankenheimer, 1977, US)
Blue Max, The (John Guillermin, 1966, US)
Born on the Fourth of July (Oliver Stone, 1989, US)
Boys in Company C, The (Sydney J. Furie, 1977, US)
Braddock: Missing in Action 3 (Aaron Norris, 1988, US)
Bridge at Remagan (John Guillermin, 1969, US)
Bridge Too Far, A (Richard Attenborough, 1977, US)
Bridges at Toko-Ri, The (Mark Robson, 1954, US)
Bright Shining Lie (Terry George, 1998, US)
Buffalo Soldiers (Gregor Jordan, 2003, US)
Bullets and Brown Eyes (Scott Sidney, 1916, US)
Buzzard's Shadow, The (Tom Ricketts, 1915, US)
Capture of a Boer Battery by the British (James H. White, 1900, UK)
Casablanca (Michael Curtiz, 1942, US)
Cast A Giant Shadow (Melville Shavelson, 1966, US)
Castle Keep (Sydney Pollack, 1969, US)
Casualties of War (Brian De Palma, 1989, US)
Catch 22 (Mike Nichols, 1970, US)
Cavalcade of Aviation (Thomas Mead and Joseph O'Brien, 1942, US)
Charge of the Austrian Lancers, The (German Mutoscope and Biograph Co., 1902, Germany)

Charlotte Gray (Gillian Armstrong, 2001, US)
China Gate (Samuel Fuller, 1957, US)
Citizens All (Edward Sloman, 1916, US)
Civilization (Reginald Barker, Thomas H. Ince and Raymond B. West, 1916, US)
Coming Home (Hal Ashby, 1978, US)
Command Decision (Sam Wood, 1948, US)
Corporal Kate (Paul Sloane, 1926, US)
Courage Under Fire (Edward Zwick, 1996, US)
Cross of Iron (Sam Peckinpah, 1977, US)
Crossfire (Anthony Maharaj, 1989, US)
Danger in the Pacific (Lewis D. Collins, 1942, US)
Dangerously They Live (Robert Florey, 1942, US)
Darby's Rangers (William Wellman, 1958, US)
Darling Lili (Blake Edwards, 1970, US)
Daughter of France (Edmund Lawrence, 1918, US)
Dawn Patrol (Howard Hawks, 1930, US)
Day After, The (Nicholas Meyer, 1983, US)
Days of Glory (Jacques Tourneur, 1944, US)
Dead of Night (Bob Clark, 1974, US)
December 7th (John Ford and Greg Tolland, 1943, US)
Deep Impact (Mimi Leder, 1998, US)
Deer Hunter, The (Michael Cimino, 1978, US)
Desperate Journey (Raoul Walsh, 1942, US)
Devil's Brigade, The (Andrew V. McLagen, 1968, US)
Dirty Dozen, The (Robert Aldrich, 1967, US)
Dive Bomber (Michael Curtiz, 1941, US)
Dog of the Regiment, A (D. Ross Lederman, 1927, US)
Dr Strangelove, Or How I Stopped Worrying and Learned to Love the Bomb
    (Stanley Kubrick, 1963, US)
Eagle and the Hawk, The (Stuart Walker, 1933, US)
Eagle Squadron (Arthur Lubin, 1942, US)
84 Charlie Mopic (Patrick Duncan, 1988, US)
Empire of the Sun (Steven Spielberg, 1987, US)
English Patient, The (Anthony Minghella, 1996, US)
Exterminator, The (James Glickenhaus, 1980, US)
Face of War, A (Eugene S. Jones, 1968, US)
Fail Safe (Stephen Frears, 2000, US)
Fall of a Nation, The (Thomas F. Dixon Jr, 1916, US)
Fighter Squadron (Raoul Walsh, 1948, US)
Fighting 69th, The (William Keighley, 1940, US)

Fighting Lady, The (Eugene Ling and John S. Martin, 1944, US)
Fighting Seabees (Edward Ludwig, 1944, US)
Firefox (Clint Eastwood, 1982, US)
First Blood (Ted Kotcheff, 1982, US)
Five Graves to Cairo (Billy Wilder, 1943, US)
Fixed Bayonets! (Samuel Fuller, 1951, US)
Flags of Our Fathers (Clint Eastwood, 2006, US)
Flight Command (Frank Borzage, 1940, US)
Flight of the Intruder (John Milius, 1991, US)
Flying Leathernecks (Nicholas Ray, 1951, US)
Fog of War, The (Errol Morris, 2004, US)
For the Boys (Mark Rydell, 1991, US)
Four Horsemen of the Apocalypse, The (Rex Ingram, 1921, US)
Frogmen, The (Lloyd Bacon, 1951, US)
From Here to Eternity (Fred Zinnemann, 1953, US)
Full Metal Jacket (Stanley Kubrick, 1987, US)
Gardens of Stone (Francis Ford Coppola, 1987, US)
German Dragoons Leaping the Hurdles (German Mutoscope and Biograph Co.,
    1902, Germany)
GI Jane (Ridley Scott, 1997, US)
Glory Brigade, The (Robert D. Webb, 1953, US)
Go For Broke (Robert Pirosh, 1951, US)
Go Tell the Spartans (Ted Post, 1977, US)
Good Guys Wear Black (Ted Post, 1977, US)
Good Morning, Vietnam (Barry Levinson, 1987, US)
Great Dictator, The (Charles Chaplin, 1940, US)
Great Santini, The (Lewis John Carlino, 1979, US)
Green Berets, The (John Wayne and Ray Kellog, 1968, US)
Guadalcanal Diary (Lewis Seiler, 1943, US)
Guilty of Treason (Felix E. Feist, 1949, US)
Guns of Navarone, The (J. Lee Thompson, 1961, US)
Guy Named Joe, A (Victor Fleming, 1943, US)
Hail, Hero (David Miller, 1969, US)
Hamburger Hill (John Irvin, 1987, US)
Hanoi Hilton, The (Lionel Chetwynd, 1987, US)
Hart's War (Gregory Hobit, 2002, US)
Heart of Humanity, The (Allen Holubar, 1919, US)
Heartbreak Ridge (Clint Eastwood, 1986, US)
Hearts of the World (D. W. Griffith, 1918, US)
Heaven and Earth (Oliver Stone, 1993, US)

Hell is For Heroes (Don Siegel, 1962, US)

Hell's Angels (Howard Hughes, 1930, US)

Immortal Sergeant, The (John M. Stahl, 1943, US)

In Again, Out Again (Al Christie, 1917, US)

In Country (Norman Jewison, 1989, US)

In the Name of the Prince of Peace (J. Searle Dawley, 1914, US)

Inchon (Terence Young, 1982, US)

Independence Day (Roland Emmerich, 1996, US)

International Squadron (Lothar Mendes and Lewis Seiler, 1941, US)

Iron Curtain (William A. Wellman, 1947, US)

J'Accuse (Abel Gance, 1919, France)

Jarhead (Sam Mendes, 2005, US)

Kaiser, The Beast of Berlin (Rupert Julian, 1918, US)

Kaiser Wilhelm and the Empress of Germany Reviewing Their Troops (Edison Co.,
     1902, US)

Kelly's Heroes (Brian G. Hutton, 1970, US)

Latino (Haskell Wexler, 1985, US)

Legion of the Condemned, The (William A. Wellman, 1928, US)

Let Us Have Peace (Ben F. Wilson, 1915, US)

Lilac Time (George Fitzmaurice, 1928, US)

Little American, The (Cecil B. DeMille, 1917, US)

Little Big Man (Arthur Penn, 1970, US)

Little Rebel, The (Harry Solter, 1911, US)

Longest Day, The (Ken Annakin, Andrew Marton and Bernhard Wicki, 1962, US)

Losers, The (Jack Starret, 1970, US)

Lost Battalion, The (Burton L. King, 1919, US)

Lost Battalion, The (Russell Mulcahy, 2001, US)

*M*A*S*H* (Robert Altman, 1970, US)

MacArthur: The Rebel General (Joseph Sargent, 1977, US)

Mad Parade, The (William Beaudine, 1931, US)

Manchurian Candidate, The (John Frankenheimer, 1962, US)

Marianne (Robert Z. Leonard, 1929, US)

Memphis Belle (William Wyler, 1944, US)

Memphis Belle (Michael Caton-Jones, 1990, US)

Men in War (Anthony Mann, 1957, US)

Menace of the Rising Sun (Henry Clay Bate and Allan F. Kitchel Jr, 1942, US)

Midnight Clear, A (Keith Gordon, 1992, US)

Midway (Jack Smight, 1976, US)

Missing (Constantin Costa-Gravas, 1984, US)

Missing in Action (Joseph Zito, 1984, US)

Missing in Action 2: The Beginning (Lance Hool, 1985, US)
Mission to Moscow (Michael Curtiz, 1943, US)
Mother Night (Keith Gordon, 1996, US)
Mulan (Tony Bancroft and Barry Cook, 1998, US)
My Four Years in Germany (William Nigh, 1918, US)
Naked and the Dead, The (Raoul Walsh, 1958, US)
Navy SEALS (Lewis Teague, 1990, US)
1941 (Steven Spielberg, 1979, US)
North Star, The (Lewis Milestone, 1943, US)
Objective Burma (Raoul Walsh, 1945, US)
On the Beach (Stanley Kramer, 1959, US)
One Minute to Zero (Tay Garnett, 1952, US)
Operation Petticoat (Blake Edwards, 1959, US)
Ordinary People (Robert Redford, 1980, US)
Paths of Glory (Stanley Kubrick, 1957, US)
Patriot, The (William S. Hart, 1916, US)
Patton: Lust for Glory (Franklin J. Schaffner, 1969, US)
Peacemaker, The (Mimi Leder, 1997, US)
Pearl Harbor (Michael Bay, 2001, US)
Perkin's Peace Party (Mutual, 1916, US)
Platoon (Oliver Stone, 1986, US)
Pork Chop Hill (Lewis Milestone, 1959, US)
Pride of the Marines (Delmer Davis, 1945, US)
Prisoner of Japan, A (Arthur Ripley, 1942, US)
Prisoner of War (Andrew Marton, 1954, US)
Purple Heart, The (Lewis Milestone, 1944, US)
Quiet American, The (Joseph L. Mankiewicz, 1958, US)
Quiet American, The (Philip Noyce, 2002, US)
Rambo: First Blood Part II (George Pan Cosmatos, 1985, US)
Rambo III (Peter MacDonald, 1988, US)
Red Dawn (John Milius, 1984, US)
Remember Pearl Harbor (Joseph Stanley, 1942, US)
Report From the Aleutians (John Huston, 1943, US)
Retreat, Hell! (Joseph H. Lewis, 1952, US)
Revenge Is My Destiny (Joseph Adler, 1971, US)
Rolling Thunder (John Flynn, 1977, US)
Rules of Engagement (William Friedkin, 2000, US)
Sahara (Zoltan Korda, 1943, US)
Salute to the Marines (Sylvan Simon, 1943, US)
Salvador (Oliver Stone, 1986, US)

Sands of Iwo Jima (Allan Dwan, 1949, US)
Saving Private Ryan (Steven Spielberg, 1998, US)
Sayonara (Joshua Logan, 1957, US)
Schindler's List (Steven Spielberg, 1993, US)
Screaming Eagles (Charles Haas, 1956, US)
Sergeant York (Howard Hawks, 1941, US)
Sgt. Bilko (Jonathan Lynn, 1996, US)
She Goes to War (Henry King, 1929, US)
Shining Through (David Seltzer, 1992, US)
Shoulder Arms (Charles Chaplin, 1918, US)
Siege, The (Edward Zwick, 1998, US)
Slaughterhouse Five (George Roy Hill, 1972, US)
Small Soldiers (Joe Dante, 1998, US)
Sniper (Luis Llosa, 1992, US)
Soldier Blue (Ralph Nelson, 1970, US)
Somewhere I'll Find You (Wesley Ruggles, 1942, US)
Song of Russia (Gregory Ratoff, 1943, US)
So Proudly We Hail (Mark Sandrich, 1943, US)
Stalag 17 (Billy Wilder, 1953, US)
Star Wars (George Lucas, 1977, US)
Steel Helmet, The (Samuel Fuller, 1951, US)
Story of GI Joe, The (William A. Wellman, 1945, US)
Strategic Air Command (Anthony Mann, 1955, US)
Streamers (Robert Altman, 1983, US)
Stripes (Ivan Reitman, 1981, US)
Sum of All Our Fears, The (Phil Alden Robinson, 2002, US)
Task Force (Delmer Davis, 1949, US)
Taxi Driver (Martin Scorsese, 1976, US)
Tearing Down the Spanish Flag (J. Stuart Blackton and Albert E. Smith, 1898, US)
Tears of the Sun (Antoine Fuqua, 2003, US)
Tell It To The Marines (George W. Hill, 1926, US)
They Were Expendable (John Ford, 1945, US)
Thin Red Line, The (Terence Malick, 1998, US)
Thirteen Days (Roger Donaldson, 2001, US)
Thirty Seconds Over Tokyo (Mervyn LeRoy, 1943, US)
Three Kings (David O. Russell, 1999, US)
Thunderbolt (John Sturges and William Wyler, 1945, US)
Tigerland (Joel Schumacher, 2002, US)
To Hell and Back (Jesse Hibbs, 1955, US)
To the Shores of Hell (Will Zens, 1966, US)

To the Shores of Tripoli (H. Bruce Humberstone, 1942, US)
Tobruk (Arthur Hiller, 1967, US)
Too Late A Hero (Robert Aldrich, 1970, US)
Top Gun (Tony Scott, 1986, US)
Tora! Tora! Tora! (Richard Fleischer, 1970, US)
Tracks (Henry Jaglom, 1976, US)
Tuskegee Airmen (Robert Markowitz, 1995, US)
Twelve O'Clock High (Henry King, 1949, US)
Twilight's Last Gleaming (Robert Aldrich, 1977, US)
U-571 (Jonathan Mostow, 2000, US)
Uncommon Valor (Ted Kotcheff, 1983, US)
Under Fire (Roger Spottiswoode, 1983, US)
Universal Soldier (Roland Emmerich, 1992, US)
Von Ryan's Express (Mark Robson, 1965, US)
Wake Island (John Farrow, 1941, US)
Walk in the Sun, A (Lewis Milestone, 1945, US)
War Brides (Herbert Brenon, 1916, US)
War is Hell (Burt Topper, 1963, US)
War Lover, The (Philip Leacock, 1962, US)
Washington at Valley Forge (Francis Ford, 1914, US)
We Were Soldiers (Randall Wallace, 2002, US)
Welcome Home Soldier Boys (Burt Topper, 1972, US)
What Did You Do In the War Daddy? (Blake Edwards, 1966, US)
What Price Glory? (Raoul Walsh, 1926, US)
When Trumpets Fade (John Irvin, 1998, US)
Where Eagles Dare (Brian G. Hutton, 1968, US)
Why Germany Must Pay (Charles Miller, 1918, US)
Who'll Stop the Rain/Dog Soldiers (Karel Reisz, 1978, US)
Wild Bunch, The (Sam Peckinpah, 1969, US)
Windtalkers (John Woo, 2002, US)
Wings (William A. Wellman, 1927, US)
With the Marines at Tarawa (Louis Hayward, 1944, US)
Womanhood, the Glory of the Nation (J. Stuart Blackton and Earle Williams, 1917, US)
Yank in Korea, A (Lew Landers, 1951, US)
Yank in the RAF, A (Henry King, 1941, US)
Yank in Viet-Nam, A (Marshall Thomspon, 1964, US)
Young Lions, The (Edward Dmytryk, 1958, US)

BIBLIOGRAPHY

Adair, G. (1981) *Hollywood's Vietnam: From The Green Berets to Apocalpyse Now*. New York: Proteus.

Allen, R. (ed.) (2000) *War Movie Posters*. New York: Hershenson.

Ambrose, S. (1994) *D-Day June 6, 1944: The Climactic Battle of World War II*. New York: Touchstone.

_____ (1997) *Citizen Soldiers*. New York: Simon and Shuster.

Anderegg, M. (ed.) (1991) *Inventing Vietnam: The War in Film and Television*. Philadelphia: Temple University Press.

Anderson, B. (1983) *Imagined Communities: Reflections on the Origin and Spread of Nationalism*. London: Verso.

Armitage, J. (2000) *Paul Virilio: From Modernism to Hypermodernism and Beyond*. London: Sage.

Aulich, J. and J. Walsh (eds) (1989) *Vietnam Images: War and Representation*. New York: St. Martin's.

Auster, A. (2002) '*Saving Private Ryan* and American Triumphalism', *Journal of Popular Film and Television*, 30, 2, 98–104.

Auster, A. and L. Quart. (1988) *How the War Was Remembered: Hollywood and Vietnam*. New York: Prager.

Basinger, J. (1986) *The World War II Combat Film: Anatomy of a Genre*. New York: Columbia University Press.

Birdwell, J. E. (1991) *Celluloid Soldiers: The Warner Bros. Campaign Against Nazism*. New York: New York University Press.

Brokaw, T. (2002) *The Greatest Generation*. London: Pimlico.

Bourke, J. (1999) *An Intimate History of Killing: Face-to-Face Killing in Twentieth Century Warfare*. London: Granta.

Bradley, J. and R. Powers (2000) *Flags of Our Fathers*. New York: Bantam Books.

Butler, I. (1974) *The War Film*. New York: A. S. Barnes.

Campbell, C. W. (1985) *Reel America and World War I.* Jefferson, NC: McFarland.

Chambers II, J. W. (1994) '*All Quiet on the Western Front* (US, 1930): The Anti-war Film and the Image of Modern War', *Historical Journal of Film, Radio and Television*, 14, 4, 377–413.

_____ (1997) 'All Quiet on the Western Front (US, 1930): The Anti-war Film and the Image of Modern War', in D. Culbert and J. W. Chambers II (eds) *World War II: Film and History.* Oxford: Oxford University Press, 13–31.

Christie, I. (1994) *The Last Machine: Early Cinema and the Birth of the Modern World.* London: BBC Educational Developments.

Collins, J. (1993) 'Genericity in the Nineties: Eclectic Irony and the New Sincerity', in J. Collins, H. Radner and A. Preacher (eds) *Film Theory Goes to the Movies.* New York: Routledge, 242–63.

Cumings, B. (1988) *Korea: The Unknown War.* New York: Random House.

_____ (1992) *War and Television.* New York: Verso.

Curley, S. J. and F. J. Wetta (eds) (1992) *Celluloid Wars: A Guide to Film and the American Experience of War.* Westport, CT: Greenwood Press.

Davenport, R. R. (2003) *The Encyclopedia of War Movies.* New York: Facts On File.

DeBauche L. (1997) *Reel Patriotism: The Movies and World War I.* Madison, WI: University of Wisconsin Press.

Dibbets, K. and B. Hogenkamp (1995) *Film and the First World War.* Amsterdam: Amsterdam University Press.

Dick, B. (1985) *The Star-Spangled Screen: The American World War II Film.* Lexington, KY: University of Kentucky Press.

Dittmar, L. and G. Michaud (eds) (1990) *From Hanoi to Hollywood: The Vietnam War in American Film.* New Brunswick, NJ: Rutgers University Press.

Doherty, T. (1993) *Projections of War: Hollywood, American Culture, and World War II.* New York: Columbia University Press.

_____ (2002) 'The New War Movies as Moral Rearmament: *Black Hawk Down* and *We Were Soldiers*', *Cineaste*, 27, 3, 4–8.

Dolan, E. F. (1985) *Hollywood Goes to War.* Twickenham: Hamlyn.

Dower, J. (1986) *War Without Mercy: Race and Power in the Pacific War.* New York: Pantheon.

Easthope, A. (1989) 'Realism and its Subversion: Hollywood and Vietnam', in J. Walsh and J. Aulich (eds) *Vietnam Images: War and Representation.* New York: St. Martin's, 30–50.

Eagleton, T. (1991) *Ideology: An Introduction.* London: Verso.

Edwards, P. M. (1997) *A Guide to Films of the Korean War.* Westport, CT: Greenwood Press.

Eisenstein, S. (1992 [1929]) 'The Cinematographic Principle and the Ideogram/A Dialectic Approach to Film Form', in G. Mast, M. Cohen and L. Braudy (eds)

Film Theory and Criticism. London: Fontana Press, 127–55.

Evans, J. (1998) *Celluloid Mushroom Clouds: Hollywood and the Atomic Bomb*. Boulder, CO: Westview.

Fore, S. (1985) 'Kuntzel's Law and *Uncommon Valour*, or Reshaping the National Consciousness in Six Minutes Flat', *Wide Angle*, 7, 4, 23–35.

Franklin, B. H. (2000) *Vietnam and Other American Fantasies*. Amherst: University of Massachusetts Press.

French, K. (2000) *Apocalypse Now*. London: Bloomsbury.

Fussell, P. (1975) *The Great War and Modern Memory*. New York: Oxford University Press.

____ (2004) *The Boys' Crusade: American GIs in Europe – Chaos and Fear in World War II*. London: Weidenfield and Nicolson.

Gledhill, C. (1987) *Home Is Where the Heart Is: Studies in Melodrama and the Woman's Film*. London: British Film Institute.

Gunning, T. (1990) 'The Cinema of Attractions: Early Film, Its Spectator and the Avant-garde', in T. Elsaesser (ed.) *Early Cinema: Space, Frame, Narrative*. London: British Film Institute, 56–63.

Hammond M. (2002) 'Some Smothering Dreams: The Combat Film in Contemporary Hollywood,' in S. Neale (ed.) *Genre and Contemporary Hollywood*. London: British Film Institute, 62–77.

Hallin, D. C. (1986) *The 'Uncensored War': The Media and Vietnam*. New York: Oxford University Press.

Hoberman, J. (1989) 'Vietnam: The Remake', in B. Kruger and P. Marians (eds) *Remaking History*. Seattle: Bay Press, 174–96.

Hodgkins, J. (2002) 'In the Wake of Desert Storm: A Consideration of Modern World War II Films', *Journal of Popular Film and Television*, 30, 2, 74–84.

Hüppauf, B. (1995) 'Modernism and the Photographic Representation of War and Destruction', in L. Devereaux and R. Hillman (eds) *Fields of Vision: Essays in Film Studies, Visual Anthropology and Photography*. Los Angeles: University of California Press, 94–124.

Hyams, J. (1984) *War Movies*. New York: Gallery Books.

Isenberg, M. T. (1981) *War on Film: The American Cinema and World War I, 1914–1941*. Rutherford: Fairleigh Dickinson University Press.

James, D. (1985) 'Presence of Discourse/Discourse of Presence: Representing Vietnam', *Wide Angle*, 7, 4, 41–53.

____ (1990) 'Rock and Roll in Representations of Vietnam', *Representations*, 29, 79–97.

Jeavons, C. (1974) *A Pictorial History of War Films*. Secaucus, NJ: The Citadel Press.

Jeffords, S. (1989) *The Remasculinizaton of America: Gender and the Vietnam War*. Bloomington, IN: Indiana University Press.

Kane, K. (1976) *Visions of War: Hollywood Combat Films of World War II*. Ann Arbor, MI: UMI Research Press.

_____ (1988) 'The World War II Combat Film', in W. D. Gehring (ed.) *Handbook of American Film Genres*. Westport, CT: Greenwood Press, 85–105.

Kagan, N. (1974) *The War Film*. New York: Pyramid Publications.

Keane, S. (2006) *Disaster Movies: The Cinema of Catastrophe* (second edition). London: Wallflower Press.

Kelly, A. (1997) *Cinema and the Great War*. London: Routledge.

Kerr, P. (1980) 'The Vietnam Subtext', *Screen*, 21, 2, 67–72.

Klein, M. (1990) 'Historical Memory, Film, and the Vietnam Era', in L. Dittmar and G. Michaud (eds) *From Hanoi to Hollywood: The Vietnam War in American Film*. New Brunswick, NJ: Rutgers University Press, 19–41.

Knightley, P. (1989) *The First Casualty: From the Crimea to Vietnam – The War Correspondent as Hero, Propagandist and Myth Maker*. London: Pan Books.

Koppes, C. R. and G. Black (1990) *Hollywood Goes to War: How Politics, Profits, and Propaganda Shaped World War Two Movies*. Berkeley, CA: University of California Press.

Krämer, P. (2006) *The New Hollywood: From Bonnie and Clyde to Star Wars*. London: Wallflower Press.

Landon, P. (1998) 'Realism, Genre and *Saving Private Ryan*', *Film and History*, 28, 3–4, 58–62.

Landy, M. (2004) 'America Under Attack': Pearl Harbor, 9/11 and History in the Media', in W. W. Dixon (ed.) *Film and Television After 9/11*. Carbondale, IL: Southern Illinois University Press, 79–101.

Langman, L. and E. Borg (eds) (1989) *Encyclopedia of American War Films*. New York: Garland.

Linville, S. E. (2000) 'The Mother of All Battles': *Courage Under Fire* and the Gender-integrated Military', *Cinema Journal*, 39, 2, 100–21.

Louvre, A. and J. Walsh (eds) (1988) *Tell Me Lies About Vietnam: Cultural Battles for the Meaning of the War*. Milton Keynes: Open University Press.

McAdams, F. (2002) *The American War Film: History and Hollywood*. Westport, CT: Praeger.

Malo, J. J. and T. Williams. (1994) *Vietnam War Films: Over 600 Feature, Made-for-TV, Pilot, and Short Films*. Jefferson, NC: McFarland.

Maltby, R. (1983) *Harmless Entertainment: Hollywood and the Ideology of Consensus*. Metuchen, NJ: Scarecrow Press.

_____ (2003) *Hollywood Cinema*. London: Blackwell.

Manvell, R. (1974) *Films and the Second World War*. New York: A. S. Barnes.

Martin, A. (1993) *Receptions of War: Vietnam in American Culture*. Norman, OK: University of Oklahoma Press.

Matelski, M. J. and N. L. Street (2003) *War and Film in America: Historical and Critical Essays*. Jefferson, NC: McFarland.

Maxim, H. *Defenseless America*. New York: Hearst's International Library Co.

Merritt, R. (1981) 'D. W. Griffith Directs The Great War: The Making of *Hearts of the World*', *Quarterly Review of Film Studies*, 6, 1, 45–67.

Moore, H. G. and J. L. Galloway (1992) *We Were Soldiers Once ... and Young: The Battle that Changed the War in Vietnam*. New York: Random House.

Morella, J., E. Z. Epstein and J. Griggs. (1973) *The Films of World War II*. Secaucus, NJ: Citadel.

Neale, S. (1980) *Genre*. London: British Film Institute.

_____ (1981) 'Genre and cinema', in T. Bennett, S. Boyd-Bowman, C. Mercer and J. Woollacott (eds) *Popular Television and Film*. London: British Film Institute, 6–25.

_____ (1991) 'Aspects of Ideology and Narrative Form in the American War Film', *Screen*, 32, 1, 35–59.

_____ (2000) *Genre and Hollywood*. London: Routledge.

Neilson, J. (1998) *Warring Fictions: Cultural Politics and the Vietnam War Narrative*. Jackson: University Press of Mississippi.

Paris, M. (1999) *The First World War and Popular Cinema: 1914 to the Present*. Edinburgh: Edinburgh University Press.

Parish, J. R. (1990) *The Great Combat Pictures: Twentieth Century Warfare on the Screen*. Metuchen, NJ: Scarecrow.

Patterson, H. (ed.) (2003) *The Cinema of Terrence Malick: Poetic Visions of America*. London: Wallflower Press.

Perlmutter, T. (1974) *War Movies*. Hamlyn: London.

Piehler, K. G. (1995) *Remembering War the American Way*. Washington DC: Smithsonian Institution Press.

Quirk, L. (1994) *The Great War Films*. New York: Citadel Press.

Renov, M. (1988) *Hollywood's Wartime Women: Representation and Ideology*. Ann Arbor, MI: UMI Research Press.

Roeder, G. H. (1993) *The Censored War: American Visual Experience During World War II*. New Haven, CT: Yale University Press.

Roper, J. (1995) 'Overcoming the Vietnam Syndrome: The Gulf War and Revisionism', in J. Walsh (ed.) *The Gulf War Did Not Happen: Politics, Culture and Warfare Post-Vietnam*. London: Arena, 27–49.

Rowe, J. C. (1986) 'Eye-witness: Documentary Styles in the American Representation of Vietnam', *Cultural Critique*, 1, 3, 126–50.

_____ (1989) 'Bringing It All Back Home': American Recyclings of the Vietnam War', in N. Armstrong and L. Tennenhouse (eds) *The Violence of Representation: Literature and the History of Violence*. London: Routledge, 197–219.

Rowe, J. C. and R. Berg (eds) (1991) *The Vietnam War and American Culture*. New York: Columbia University Press.

Rubin, S. J. (1981) *Combat Films: American Realism, 1945–1970*. Jefferson, NC: McFarland.

Ryan, M. and D. Kellner (1988) *Camera Politica: The Politics and Ideology of Contemporary American Film*. Bloomington, IN: Indiana University Press.

Schatz, T. (1998) 'World War II and the Hollywood 'War Film', in N. Browne (ed.) *Refiguring American Film Genres: History and Theory*. Berkeley, CA: University of California Press, 89–128.

Selig, M. (1993) 'Genre, Gender and the Discourse of War: The A-historical and Vietnam films', *Screen*, 31, 1, 1–19.

Shain, R. E. (1976) *An Analysis of Motion Pictures About War Released by the American Film Industry*. New York: Arno Press.

Shindler, C. (1979) *Hollywood Goes To War: Films and American Society, 1939–1952*. London: Routledge and Kegan Paul.

Shull, M. S and D. E. Wilt. (1996) *Hollywood War Films, 1937–1945: An Exhaustive Filmography of American Feature-Length Motion Pictures Relating to World War II*. Jefferson, IL: McFarland.

Slide, A. (1994) *Early American Cinema*. Metuchen, NJ: Scarecrow Press.

Sobchack, V. (1984) 'Inscribing Ethical Space: Ten Propositions On Death, Representation and Documentary', *Quarterly Review of Film Studies*, 9, 4, 283–300.

Sontag, S. (2003) *Regarding the Pain of Others*. London: Hamish Hamilton.

Sorlin, P. (1994) 'War and Cinema: Interpreting the Relationship', *Historical Journal of Film, Radio and Television*, 14, 4, 357–66.

_____ (2000) 'Cinema and the Memory of the Great War', in M. Paris (ed.) *The First World War and Popular Cinema*. New Brunswick, NJ, 5–26.

Springer, C. (1988) 'Anti-war Film As Spectacle: Contradictions of the Combat Sequence', *Genre*, 21, 4, 479–86.

Sturken, M. (1997) *Tangled Memories: The Vietnam War, the AIDS Epidemic, and the Politics of Remembering*. Berkeley, CA: University of California Press.

Suid, L. H. (1978) *Guts & Glory: Great American War Movies*. Reading, MA: Addison-Wesley.

Taylor, J. (1998) *Body Horror: Photojournalism, Catastrophe and War*. Manchester: Manchester University Press.

Tasker, Y. (1993) *Spectacular Bodies: Gender, Genre and the Action Cinema*. London: Routledge.

Tindall, G. B. and D. E. Shi. (2000) *America: A Narrative History*. New York: W. W. Norton.

Torry, R. (1993) 'Therapeutic Narrative: *The Wild Bunch*, *Jaws* and Vietnam', *The Velvet Light Trap*, 31, 27–38.

Turner, F. (1996) *Echoes of Combat: The Vietnam War in American Memory*. New York: Anchor.

Virilio, P. (1989) *War and Cinema: The Logistics of Perception*. New York: Verso.

Walsh, J. (1988) '*First Blood* to *Rambo*: A Textual Analysis', in A. Louvre and J. Walsh (eds) *Tell Me Lies About Vietnam: Cultural Battles for the Meaning of the War*. Milton Keynes: Open University Press, 50–62.

Woll, A. L. (1982) *The Hollywood Musical Goes to War*. Chicago: Nelson.

Wood, R. (1986) *Hollywood from Vietnam to Reagan*. New York: Columbia University Press.

Young, M. B. (1991) *The Vietnam Wars 1945–1990*. New York: HarperCollins.

_____ (1995) 'The War's Tragic Legacy', in R. J. McMahon (ed.) *Major Problems in the History of the Vietnam War*. Lexington, MA: D. C. Heath, 637–47.

INDEX